PRAISE FOR
DAVID KLASS'S
CALIFORNIA BLUE:

"Klass writes a sort of enriched sports fiction, combining vividly told stories of athletic competition with perceptive explorations of character and social themes. This is his best work yet. . . . A rich story, capped by a brilliantly crafted, multi-layered reconciliation. . . ."
— *Kirkus Reviews*, pointed review

"This is the story of a young man caught up in some large and passionate issues before he is ready to cope with them. . . . But this novel's strength does not lie simply in its willingness to tackle big issues. Small scenes . . . are well done and add to the novel's texture and depth. A thoughtful and fair book. . . ."
— *School Library Journal*, starred review

"In this beautifully rendered novel, Klass . . . transforms an abstract environmental issue into a compelling story of a boy in transition from adolescence to adulthood . . . . absorbing. . . ."
— *Publishers Weekly*

CALIFORNIA
BLUE

*Rafael
Dello-Strologo*

CALIFORNIA BLUE

David Klass

SCHOLASTIC INC.
New York Toronto London Auckland Sydney

For Aaron M. Priest,
a wonderful agent and a true friend

No part of this publication may be reproduced in whole or in part, or stored in a retrieval system, or transmitted in any form or by any means, electronic, mechanical, photocopying, recording, or otherwise, without written permission of the publisher. For information regarding permission, write to Scholastic Inc., 555 Broadway, New York, NY 10012.

ISBN 0-590-46689-5

24 23 22 21 20 19 18 17 16 15 14 13   2/0

Printed in the U.S.A.   01

Chapter
One

I don't know why running through a redwood forest has always made me think of death.

It's not because I grew up in a mill town — I don't run between the trees seeing five-hundred-foot-tall piles of sawdust or neatly stacked lumber or endless reams of paper. And it's not because of the darkness where the old growth is thickest, although as I pounded along the narrow forest trail, the massive trees pressed in against each other in the twilight, and the smell of the wood and leaves was damp and lightly sweet and faintly bloodlike.

I was well into the heart of the old growth now, with the great trunks rising around me like massive pillars of a giant cathedral. High overhead, the forest ceiling was vaulted with dark branches and latticed with leaves that blotted out the purple light of the sinking sun.

I fell into my six-minute-mile pace. This is a comfortable rhythm for me, a little faster than a jog and a little slower than team practice laps. I can lose myself in a six-minute-mile pace and just keep pumping with my arms and legs while my mind floats free to ponder the large and small mysteries of the universe. In a redwood forest, the mysteries are mostly large.

I guess redwoods make me think of death because of their size and age. I'm used to thinking of myself as kind of important, and the trees give me a different perspective. Some of the great sequoias deep in the old growth were seedlings when Socrates drank hemlock, and saplings when Julius Caesar crossed the Rubicon. They grew to several hundred feet during the Dark Ages, and there they stand today, in exactly the same cool forest glade they have grown in for millennia while human history has gone on and on in other corners of the globe.

I've just turned seventeen, and running through a forest of three-hundred-foot-tall living creatures, some of them more than a hundred times older than I am, helps me remember that the human lifespan is a brief one. If we don't cut them all down, these trees will be growing in exactly the same spring-fed glade when my grandson's grandson is training for his high school track team or whatever guys will be doing in the twenty-second century to earn varsity letters and impress girls.

I like to run alone. It's best when there's a slight chill in the air. My favorite time to run is in the late afternoon, when the clouds seem to swim toward sunset, and the enormous shadows from the tree trunks thicken and begin to merge into a wall of darkness.

Sometimes I run in my track team shorts and T-shirt, pretending it's the county championship race and I'm out in front. The leaves rustle overhead, and

I make believe it's applause and pick up the pace. "John, John, John!" I fly into a full sprint and the birdcalls become whistles from the crowd and the narrow forest trail turns into a cinder track with a ribbon stretched across the far distance for the winner.

Sometimes I carry a pack on my back, with a collapsible rod and some flies, and stop at Thompson's Creek for a little fishing. You can catch trout up to about fifteen inches long in the pools beneath the falls. I used to bring them home and clean them and eat them, but now I catch them and let them go.

Sometimes I take my net.

On this particular Wednesday I had my racket net with me, and a small collecting jar. I also had a very real reason for thinking about death as I started the slight uphill stretch that would take me past Thompson's Creek to the hole in the fence by Highlook Lane.

It had been a rough forty-eight hours, and I can't tell you how good it felt to fall into my six-minute-mile rhythm and lose myself on the forest trail. It's okay to think about death when you're running through a forest, alone, at twilight. It's quite another thing to meet it face to face at your dinner table, over a plate of grilled lamb chops.

Two days ago, almost as soon as we sat down to dinner, I could tell that something was very wrong. There was a tension in the room that I couldn't identify, but it floated just above the table, as palpable as the aroma of mashed potatoes and grilled lamb and green beans. My mother was talking too much, and my father wasn't saying anything at all.

Usually it's the other way around. Dad questions me in annoying detail about how school went and how my training is going. My mother, on the other hand, prefers to listen. I've seen her at family gatherings go from hour to hour and from conversation to conversation, listening and smiling and obviously enjoying herself, but never saying a single word.

Two nights ago, she couldn't keep quiet. "I hope I didn't burn the lamb. I know you both like it a little pink, but I'm afraid it's not cooked through. I cut off a sliver to see, and it looked okay, but I don't want either of you getting sick . . ." She stopped abruptly, picked up her water glass, and took a couple of quick sips.

"It tastes like you always make it," I told her.

"Well, the price is so high," she said, continuing a thought that she hadn't started. "It's really something of a luxury. But I know how much you both like lamb chops. Once in a while we deserve a treat."

She took another quick sip of water and plunged right on. "I saw a homeless family in front of the supermarket today. The man held a sign saying he was willing to work for food. And the woman held her baby. I wanted to give them a dollar, but all I could spare was some change. I felt so sorry for them. I wonder where they sleep? I hope the baby has enough to eat. It made me feel guilty, buying so many things, but it also made me worry because if it could happen to them, it could happen to anyone. They looked like decent people who had just had some bad breaks. I don't know what we'll do if prices keep rising this way."

"Is something wrong?" I asked her. "Are we suddenly poor? I don't get it."

She took a quick forkful of mashed potatoes. The lines in her face deepened as she chewed and swallowed, and suddenly she veered off once again in a totally new direction. "I ran into Miss Merrill at the supermarket, and she said the prom's going to be at the high school this year. She said it's because they're short of money, but I think it's a nice change."

Mom's voice dropped down to a whisper, but she kept talking so quickly that her sentences almost ran together. "I never liked the idea of having the prom in a hotel. It was at the school gym for years. The gym was good enough for us. When they decorate it with balloons and crepe paper, it looks very nice. I hope you're going to ask someone, John. Miss Merrill said that lots of juniors are going. I'm sure there are plenty of girls who would like to go with you."

"Sure," I mumbled. "Hundreds."

But she wasn't even listening to me. She was looking at my father in a very peculiar way. "Do you remember our prom, Henry? I was looking at the pictures the other day. I still remember most of the songs they played. You were so handsome. When you came to pick me up, I think that was the first time I ever saw you in a suit and tie."

In seventeen years of eating dinner at this table, I had never seen my mother talk so much. I couldn't figure it out. Suddenly she put her fork down and picked up a napkin. She lifted it to her face as if to dab her lips, and it took me a minute to realize that she was crying.

My father put a gentle hand on her shoulder. "Meg," he said. "Don't." It was halfway between a request and a command.

She nodded, but she couldn't stop crying. "I'm

sorry," she said. She stood up from the table. "Please keep eating. I'm sorry. Excuse me for a minute. Please, finish the lamb and take seconds. Don't if it's too pink, but if it's not, eat as much as you want. Excuse me."

"Mom, what's wrong?"

"Nothing," she said, and ran out of the dining room.

There was a long, strange silence. I looked at my father. He went on eating, sawing off neat pieces of lamb, dipping them in mashed potatoes and gravy, and then popping them into his mouth. He didn't look up at me till I said, "Did you and Mom have a fight?"

"Nope."

"Well, something's wrong. Aren't you going to go see what it is?"

"I'm going to finish my dinner." He popped another piece of grilled lamb into his mouth, chewed, and swallowed.

I stood up. "I'm going to see what's wrong with her."

"Nothing's wrong with your mother."

"She just ran out of here crying. Don't you think something must be wrong with her?"

"With me."

"What?"

"Not with her. With me."

"You know what this is all about?"

"Sit back down." Once again, it was halfway between a request and a command.

I sat. "What's going on?"

Dad looked up from his plate, and we studied each other in silence for a long minute. We've never gotten along very well. Everybody says he's a perfect father, so I guess it must be my fault. Almost since I can remember, every time he's tried to push me one way, I've gone in the other direction. I can't say exactly why. All my brothers and sisters turned out exactly the way he wanted and they all seem to be leading perfect lives. I've got two older sisters who were cheerleaders, and two older brothers who were high school football stars. All four of them finished high school, got married, found good jobs, and are very happy.

I'm the youngest, by almost five years. I think I must have been a mistake. They had had four wonderful kids and they didn't plan on having any more, and then my mom got pregnant with me and they decided, "Oh, what the heck, why not?"

I guess they wish they had quit at four.

My dad still holds the record for most yards gained by a Kiowa High School football player. There's a plaque in the trophy case in school that lists all the major school records, and his name is at the very top: Henry Arthur Rodgers, 2,111 yards, 1954–57. It's kind of intimidating to think how many strong and fleet kids before and since have taken their best shot and fallen short of Henry Arthur Rodgers.

I didn't even try. During the football season I run cross-country. During the basketball season I run indoor track. And, of course, during the baseball season, when my father thinks I should be digging hard ground balls out of the dirt and sliding headfirst into home, I run track.

Now his heavily muscled arms were on the table, a fork in his left hand, his right a loosely folded fist near his spoon.

"What is it?" I asked him.

"Bad news."

"Tell me something I don't know."

He smiled. His face looks like a sculptor carved a bust of the perfect hard-working American man for some sort of blue collar hall of fame. He's got a cleft chin, a small mouth, high cheekbones, and intense black eyes. His hair is thinning a bit near the temples, and a few white hairs can be seen in the dark tangle on top. I don't think he's ever had even an inch of paunch all through middle age. Dad looks like he could still gain a hundred yards in a high school game if you dressed him up in pads and handed him the football. Now, watching me carefully, he lowered his fork. "Thirty percent," he said.

"What are you talking about?"

"That's why your mother's crying. Thirty percent."

"Of what?"

"I went for some tests. Haven't been feeling so good lately. Got the results today." My father didn't look away or change his tone in the slightest. "Doctor says I've got a thirty-percent chance."

"Of what?"

His right fist flattened out on the tabletop. The silence was so deep that I could hear my mother sobbing softly in the kitchen.

"Of what? Tell me."

"Leukemia." The word seemed unnatural on his lips, and he replaced it quickly with some shorter ones. "Cancer of the blood. The doctor gives me a thirty-percent chance. That's why your mother's so upset. It's only going to get rougher around here

8

before it gets better, so I think the best thing we can do is learn to finish our dinners."

It felt like a sledgehammer had just swung down on the center of my forehead. I sat there waiting for the world to take on some kind of a normal focus again. My mother came back into the room, drying her eyes, and we looked at each other. Then, as if on cue, we both looked at my father, who went back to eating his lamb, slowly and deliberately, each bite exactly the same size as the ones before it.

The dinner scene of two days before receded as I swerved to avoid a fallen branch in the middle of the forest trail. I had been lost deep, deep in my six-mile-a-minute pace, so it was a bit of a shock to reemerge suddenly in the sweet gloom of the redwood forest. I knew I must be nearing the creek, so I picked up my pace just a little and sped down the gentle slope.

You can hear Thompson's Creek about a hundred feet before you see it. The gossiping of the leaves with the breeze takes on an urgency till you feel there must be a new presence in the forest, whispering new and different secrets, and then as you get real close you can make out the splash of the waterfall scattering silver current between sharp rocks. At its widest point, it's twenty feet apart — in places, it's less than ten. There's a log bridge a little farther upstream, but everyone I know picks their way across on stepping-stones, occasionally slipping and dipping their feet in the water.

I slowed to an easy jog and then to a walk, and stopped near the side of the creek. I could see my reflection clearly in the gently rippling mirror. To tell the truth, I've never liked the way I look very much, even reflected in a creek bed. I'm tall and thin — I guess gawky is the right word. My sandy brown hair is uncombable and sticks out in all angles and directions, like roofing thatch. I hate my nose. It's sharp and small like a beak, and I think it gives people a bad first impression of me. It makes me look serious and mean. All the other males in my family are friendly-looking and very handsome — I can't imagine how my genes got so screwed up.

Kneeling and reaching down with both hands, I scooped up some water and splashed it over my face. The spring that feeds Thompson's Creek originates high up in the glaciers of the Sierra, and all year round the water is ice-cold. My cheeks and chin tingled as the freezing water dripped back into the creek and fractured my reflection.

Above the center of the creek the tree cover parted, and dusky light sailed down the falls and flooded the forest floor. I picked my way carefully across the stones to the far bank, and cut through the dense underbrush. Prickly toothed sow thistles nipped at my legs. I spotted a few yellow hawkbit flowers, and a giant patch of western azaleas already in full bloom. Flitting above the azaleas, I was amazed to see what looked like a Mustard White, playfully zigzagging back and forth and up and down on the evening breeze.

Mustard Whites are a lot more common in the Cascades and the mountains of British Columbia than in northern California. But there the little sucker was above the azaleas, and there I was a few feet away with my net and collecting jar. I held the net ready in my right hand and stepped a little closer.

It was a Mustard White beyond any doubt; I could see the wings clearly, and there were no dark spots on the uppersides. It wasn't the first one I had ever seen in this forest, but it was the first one I had ever tried to catch.

I swiped and missed. The butterfly rose up about ten feet from the ground and leisurely headed north. I cut through the dense underbrush, following it and waiting for another chance. The going was tough, but the chase was a welcome respite from my worries about what was waiting for me at home. Twice I jumped up and swiped at the butterfly, and twice it eluded me. It flew on, and I ran on beneath it. We were having a nice little game, and the Mustard White was winning.

Finally it came down, about fifteen feet ahead of me. Recklessly I charged forward, my net raised. I was paying so much attention to the butterfly that I didn't see the ground fall away suddenly in a ten-foot drop disguised by branches and bushes. I sprinted right off the edge of the drop, waved my net once, futilely, at the Mustard White, which hovered just beyond my reach, and then I plummeted.

A bush cushioned my landing, but even so, the impact knocked me senseless. When my mind cleared, I sat up and took stock. My arms and legs didn't seem to be broken. Some small branches had cut my face a little, and my hands and wrists were scratched up, but all in all it had been a lucky landing.

There was no sign of the Mustard White.

I got to my feet and glanced down at the buckeye bush that had broken my fall. I had nearly flattened it. If plants can think, this one must have been curs-

11

ing its luck. As I glanced down at it, rubbing myself off, I saw the chrysalis.

At first I didn't recognize it as a chrysalis. I saw peculiar white streaks on a leaf and pulled away. They looked like bird droppings, and I was afraid I might have rubbed against them and gotten my clothes dirty. Then I took a closer look and realized that they were chrysalises — not just one, but at least a half a dozen. The white streaks that resembled bird droppings were clearly natural camouflage.

It's not unusual for butterfly chrysalises to use camouflage or to have other elaborate ways of hiding. Many moths go through their pupal stage underground, but almost all butterflies go through their metamorphosis above ground, within reach of all sorts of predators and particularly hungry birds. So butterfly chrysalises have evolved fascinating ways to avoid being eaten. Some species such as the Adonis Blue hide in leaf litter on the forest floor. Erebia Ringlet pupae are encased in protective silk cocoons. Many species' chrysalises have shapes and colors that resemble leaves and twigs. There's even a kind of butterfly, called the Green Hairstreak, whose chrysalises make threatening sounds when they're disturbed.

I'd heard of caterpillars with markings that looked like bird droppings, but never a chrysalis. I gently snapped off a twig with one of the curious inch-long pupae and put it in my collecting jar. It seemed a poor replacement for the Mustard White that I had missed, but you never know exactly what kind of butterfly will eventually emerge.

It was growing dark quickly. I had chased the Mustard White nearly half a mile into the undergrowth, and I had very little idea where I was. Getting lost in a forest at night is not fun at all, so I set off quickly in what I thought must be the right direction. Luckily the fall hadn't done any serious damage, and I was able to make pretty good time. Soon I heard the gurgle of the creek and the steady wash-wash of the falls, and I knew I was going to be okay.

Of course I'd be a little late for dinner, but as my father had predicted, things seemed to be getting rougher and rougher at my home. Coming home late and missing some of the strained silences didn't seem like a totally bad idea. I turned onto the path that leads to Highlook Lane and began to jog.

Chapter Two

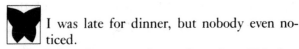I was late for dinner, but nobody even noticed.

My father always gets home from the mill before six and likes to eat at seven on the dot. I arrived home at about twenty after seven, expecting to be yelled at, and instead found a big dinner for seven all laid out but no sign of my father.

My brother Glenn had driven down from Portland with his wife, and my sister Katie had come up from Sonoma with her husband. I showered and changed, and then joined the little crowd of family members that kept moving nervously back and forth between the kitchen and the dining room.

Glenn is a little less than five years older than I am, and about a hundred times more mature. At twenty-two, when most kids his age are finishing college, he owns his own auto body shop in Tillamook, just west of Portland. He started the business with money he saved from working part-time all through high school. He's a few inches shorter than my father; he inherited Dad's muscular build and handsome looks, and particularly the same sharp black eyes.

When I walked into the kitchen, Glenn was trying to calm my mother down. "He'll be home any minute. There's no reason to get so upset."

"I should call the police," she said. "He's never this late."

"Go ahead and call them if you want, but I'm sure he's okay."

"Then why isn't he home?"

"He got tied up somewhere."

"I called the mill. They say he left at the usual time."

"Maybe he had to run an errand or drop something off somewhere."

"Why didn't he call?"

"I'm sure there's a good reason. He'll walk through the door any second."

At nine, she called the police. They said it didn't sound like anything serious, but they'd put Dad's name and description and license plate number out on the police radio. They said if Dad didn't come home by ten, we should call again and they'd send a patrolman.

We ate a silent and grim dinner without him. The cod was overcooked, and instead of family banter there was just the scraping of forks on plates and the chewing of five mouths. Mom sat with us, but she didn't eat a thing. Every few minutes she'd get up and walk to the front window and peer out at the dark driveway.

After dinner we sat in the living room, watching the hands turn on the grandfather clock and exchanging small talk. At a few minutes before ten, car headlights threw two large white ovals on the front curtains. Mom stood up from her rocker and stepped toward the door. Dad's Chevy screeched to a stop, the headlights went black, the engine switched off, and in a minute my father walked through the front door as if it were the most natural thing in the world to come home four hours late from work.

He smiled at my mother, and then noticed Glenn and Katie and their spouses. For a moment, he seemed taken aback by the little crowd that stared at him. Then he smiled. "Hey, hey, look who's here. What a great surprise." He shook Glenn's hand and kissed Katie and greeted his son- and daughter-in-law. As he passed me, I caught a strong scent of alcohol on his breath. "I hope you didn't wait dinner."

"We just finished," Glenn told him.

"Good, good. What brings you all to this neck of the woods?"

There was a short silence. "We just wanted to see how you were doing," Katie finally said in a half-whisper.

"Me?" Dad seemed incredulous. "No need to make a fuss about me."

"We didn't come to make a fuss," Glenn said. "You look great."

"I'm fine. Don't worry about me. Everything's going to be just fine. I talked to Stanley in the mill office. I told him what the doctor said and how I might have to go to San Francisco for treatment and all. He was damned decent about it. Damned decent." Dad slurred his words a little bit, and I wondered how much he had drunk. I had never seen him drink anything more than a beer or two.

"Do you want to sit down?" Katie asked him.

"Very damned decent," Dad went on, as if he hadn't heard her. "Told me not to worry about a thing. 'I'll handle this myself,' he said. 'Any time you need off, you come and tell me. Any questions you have about medical benefits and stuff like that, you come straight to me. If our insurance carrier gives you any hassle, I'll handle it myself.'" Dad swayed slightly, and then caught himself and stood upright with visible effort. "He's a stand-up guy, just like his father was."

"That was good of Stanley," my mother said softly. "Why don't you come in and sit down? I'll warm up some fish . . ."

"He said, 'You've given us thirty good years.' Actually, it's been thirty-three since I started, but thirty's close enough." For a moment, Dad lost his train of thought and stood in awkward silence. He fumbled with his hand on his shirt front, as if trying to do a button that was already buttoned. "Thirty-three years," he finally repeated. "Not thirty. Anyway, he was damned decent."

"Aren't you going to have some dinner?" Mom asked him.

"No, thanks. I'm not hungry."

Mom couldn't help asking: "Did you stop somewhere for dinner? Is that why you're so late?"

"I just got tied up at the mill, is all," Dad mumbled. "Had some work to finish. Just not hungry is all. Why are you all looking at me like that?"

When he asked us why we were looking at him,

we all looked away at the same time. My eyes locked onto a charcoal sketch of two thrushes that my mother had done years ago, and that hung near the stairs. Mom's got a very good eye — the birds were drawn in natural poses and wonderful detail. Sometimes I think she could sell her drawings professionally if she wanted to, but it's hard enough just to get her to hang a few in our house.

"Wouldn't you like a piece of cod and some potatoes?" my mother asked him again.

"Didn't I already say no?" he snapped back, a little too loudly. "Why do you ask me things after I've already answered them?"

"I'm sorry."

"You confuse me when you do that."

"I'm sorry."

"Damn it, why do you all keep staring at me?" he demanded, wheeling around toward us and moving his right hand in a sweeping gesture that upset a chair. "Is there something about me that's so interesting to look at?"

Katie bent down and righted the chair.

"We didn't mean to stare at you," Glenn said. "We drove down to give you some support and to let you know we're here for you if you need us. That's all."

My father wiped his forehead and nodded. "Sure," he said. "Look, I'm sorry. I've had a hard day. Let me just go wash my face. I'll be back in a minute."

He hurried up the stairs, holding the banister for support, and we all looked at each other. My mother went up after him, and neither of them came back down all night.

I did some homework and was just about ready

to go to bed when a knock sounded on my bedroom door. I opened it and was very surprised to see Glenn standing there. We've never been close, even though we're brothers. I think Glenn always saw me as somewhere between a nerd and a wimp, and I always thought he worked a little too hard at fitting in and being the perfect all-American male. Anyway, I was surprised to see him in my doorway. "Hey," he said.

"Hey."

"What's up?"

"Just finished some homework."

"Anything interesting?"

"Trigonometry."

"Better you than me."

"To tell you the truth, I don't like it much, either," I told him.

He smiled. "Aren't you gonna invite me in?"

I kicked the door open, and he walked in and pulled it shut behind him. He seemed uncomfortable in my little bedroom, and glanced around at the shelves overflowing with books. "You read all these?"

"Most of them."

"For school?"

"Pleasure, too."

"Got anything you think I might like?"

I can't remember ever seeing Glenn read a book. "Let me think about it," I said.

He walked over to my terrarium and looked down inquisitively at the chrysalis I had brought back from the forest. "What the hell is that?"

"A pupa."

"Sounds like something that belongs in a Kleenex."

"It's gonna hatch into a butterfly."

19

"Why do you keep it under those lamps?"

"They'll make it hatch a little bit sooner."

"What are you going to do with it after it hatches?"

"Let it go."

"You go to all the trouble of catching it, keeping it safe and under special lamps, and then you're just gonna let it go?"

"That's right."

"Seems like a waste of time."

"What do you want me to do with it? Eat it?"

"At least that would make some sense," he said. "Although it probably wouldn't taste very good."

"Lots of people in other countries eat insect larvae."

"That doesn't mean they taste good." He scowled down at the chrysalis. Glenn's a very straightforward guy, and I could see from his face that he was trying to imagine how it would taste. "You ever cut one of these things open?"

"Once or twice."

"Whatta they look like inside?"

"Noodle soup."

He turned away from the terrarium in disgust. "I don't know why you'd want something like that in your bedroom."

"I find it interesting."

"It's not normal."

A tiny edge crept into my voice. "I don't care that much about being normal."

"Well, maybe you should care a little more."

"And maybe you should care a little less. Anyway, if that's what you came into my room to tell me, then thanks for the advice, and good-night."

"Actually, I came to ask you if you'd like to take a walk."

"A walk?"

"Yeah."

"Outside?"

"It wouldn't be much fun just walking through our house."

"Isn't it kind of late?"

"If you don't want to, that's okay," he said. "Sorry to bother you."

He stepped toward the door.

"Wait a minute," I told him. "Let me get a jacket."

Chapter Three

It was a cold and perfectly clear night, with a sky full of tiny stars glittering against the darkness like snowflakes on black satin. A north wind blew with enough force so that when we walked into it, it made my eyes tear. Without speaking a word, we turned the corner onto Grayling Drive, and the wind became less punishing. Every thirty feet or so, streetlights cast nets of yellowish radiance onto the empty street.

"So," Glenn finally said, "how's school?"

"Fine."

"Getting straight A's?"

"A couple of B's."

"Mom says you're thinking about college."

"If I can get a scholarship."

"Where do you wanna go?"

I hesitated. "Maybe to an East Coast school."

"Pretty fancy." It sounded like a veiled criticism.

"I'll have to see where I get in, and if anyone offers me anything," I told him.

A pickup truck rolled by, and we watched its taillights dwindle to red cinders in the distance.

"How's the girl situation?" Glenn asked. It was like he had a checklist of items to ask about to test whether I was a normal seventeen-year-old or not. Next would probably come sports.

I didn't answer right away. Glenn had always been amazing with girls, and I had always been awful. My lack of success was mostly due to cowardice and severe awkwardness. When I'm around a girl I like, I manage to find exactly the stupidest possible thing to say, or precisely the most embarrassing thing to do. It's like I'm trapped in a Three Stooges movie. Once, last year, I got up the nerve to sit down at a school cafeteria table with a girl I had liked for a long time and a few of her friends. Somehow, in the process of sitting down, I kicked out a table leg. The table collapsed, drinks and lunches flew into the air, and I skipped eating lunch for the next week or two. That's kind of par for the course. "It's okay," I finally mumbled.

"Does that mean you have a girlfriend?"

"No."

"Anything on the horizon?"

"Glenn, lay off. Just worry about yourself."

"Okay," he said. "Sorry. It's just that there are a lot of nicer things to bring to your bedroom than bug cocoons."

"I said lay off."

We turned the corner onto Cottonwood Lane. Now, the wind was at our backs, pushing us forward. We reached the oldest part of town, where more than two hundred tiny houses had been built by the mill, all according to the same plan. They were one-story wood-frame cottages, with small lawns cut by gravel walks that connected front doors to the narrow street.

"Sorry," Glenn said. "I really mean it. I didn't ask you to come for a walk just to fight with you. I don't know why we always argue."

"It's okay," I told him. Our footsteps thumped off the dark pavement. "Actually, there is someone at school I like, but she'd never go out with me."

He seemed surprised and pleased that I would share such information with him. "Why not? Have you told her you like her?"

I shook my head.

"That might be a good way to start."

"It would also be a good way to end."

"She'd probably be thrilled. I get on your case all the time because I'm your brother, but you have an awful lot of things going for you," he said.

"There are more going against me."

"She's going out with someone else?"

"That's not the problem." I'd been wanting to talk about it with somebody for a long time, but I knew he would only laugh at me. "You'll think I'm crazy if I tell you."

"I promise I won't."

"You won't tell anyone?"

"This is ridiculous. Okay, I promise. Come on, who is she?"

"My biology teacher."

He tried to disguise a low chuckle as a cough, but finally his laugh burst out from behind his hand. "You're crazy," he said.

"I know, but I can't help it. She's only twenty-three. And she's not married. I'm her best student."

"At least now I know why you study so hard," Glenn said, still laughing. "You really like her?"

I nodded.

"For how long?"

"Months."

"Then tell her."

"If you think I'm crazy, what will she think?"

"Probably that you're crazy, too, but at least you'll have told her. You can't go through life trying to figure women out. The best thing to do is to be as truthful as possible, and try not to think too much about how they'll react."

"Okay," I said. "I'll keep that in mind."

We passed Kiowa High School. It had been built by the mill in the 1950's when the lumber business was booming. Now, like the industry that had paid for it, the two-story school building looked outdated and in poor condition. The north wind howled around the edges of the building, and the big HOME OF THE KIOWA BRAVES sign out in front creaked back and forth on its support chains.

Beyond the school, we followed the side of the athletic field. The oval outline of the track that I raced on was right next to the dark rectangle of football gridiron. Glenn stopped and peered out at the patch of grass on which he had won local fame as a halfback. "Dad says you've been winning races."

"I came in second twice," I told him.

"You would have made a great wide receiver."

"I doubt it. I'm a distance runner, not a sprinter. And I weigh a hundred and forty-eight pounds. One good tackle would have snapped my spine."

"I played as low as one sixty-five."

"It isn't my game, Glenn. I used to love to watch you, though. I remember your senior year — when you ran with the ball — everyone in the stands went crazy."

"Ah, I was just okay," Glenn said. "Seems like a lifetime ago. You don't hear too much applause when you're taking the dents out of people's cars."

I was very surprised. It was the first time I had ever heard Glenn come close to expressing some dissatisfaction with his life. He's the kind of gung-ho optimist who will force himself to say something upbeat even in the face of pure misery. "But most of the time you like what you do?"

"It's a job. It pays okay. I'm my own boss. I guess I'm lucky." He broke off, and we cut across the track to the sideline of the football field. We headed onto the field, and our feet swished through the ankle-length grass. "I wish I could have seen Dad play," Glenn whispered. "He must've really been one tough little sucker."

Now, at least, we were talking about what I knew was the real reason for this walk. "Two thousand one hundred and eleven yards," I whispered back.

"That plaque's still there?"

"I see it every day."

"Am I still fifth?"

"Yup."

"Not bad, huh?"

"For someone who played as low as one sixty-five."

"I spit a lot of blood to get on that plaque."

"I know you did."

"You must think it's pretty stupid putting yourself

through such torture just to get your name in a school trophy case."

"I couldn't do it, but I admire you for it."

"Dad's not that much bigger than I am. He must've been the toughest little sucker around in his day. Or in any other day, for that matter."

"Not these days," I said, to get it out in the open.

We walked under the goalposts and stood in the end zone, looking back up the whole length of the field, as if waiting for a kickoff. "You're talking about tonight?" Glenn asked.

"It was pretty rough."

Glenn sounded surprised. "On who?"

"All of us. Especially Mom." Glenn was watching me as if he didn't quite understand what I was saying. "I mean, he could have at least explained where he was."

"I thought he did. He's worked at the same job for thirty-three years. Today he had to go in and tell them that he'd be leaving soon and probably not be coming back."

"So?"

"It wasn't easy for him to do that. So after he left the mill, he went out and had a drink."

"He could barely stand up when he got home."

"John, our father's probably going to die," Glenn said, and the north wind blew right through me. "That means a lot of different things for our family, but one thing it means is that you'd better grow up pretty soon."

My fists clenched, and I think he saw my anger.

"You're the one at home. You're the one who's got to be there when Mom and Dad need you. The rest

27

of us will do what we can, but we've moved away and we can't move back. So you're the one."

I answered him quickly, in anger. "Dad and I have never been close, and I'm not gonna pretend we have been just because he's so sick. You say that you're on my case a lot, but it's nothing to what he's given me day after day for years. After you moved out, it got worse. Nothing I ever do is right in his eyes, or good enough for him. In his mind I'm a complete failure — the son who didn't measure up. And he knows how he makes me feel, but he keeps rubbing it in, anyway. Every damned day." I took a breath. "I'll be there for him now, if he needs me and if he treats Mom decently. He's gotta try a little harder than he did tonight."

"What's that supposed to mean?"

"He can't just feel nostalgia about leaving his job, and get drunk and not call so that everyone's worried sick."

"It wasn't nostalgia about his job." Glenn was controlling himself, but I could tell by his voice that he was really very angry at me.

"Sure it was. You heard him say it."

"That's not what's bugging him."

"Then what?"

Glenn didn't answer for a long time, but just looked down at the clumps of dark grass. Finally he said, "He's a strong, strong man, and for the first time in his life, he's scared."

"Of dying?"

"I bet he's never been afraid of anything before, and he doesn't know what to do. Looks to me like he's damn near terrified. So, don't think so much about yourself and Mom and the rest of us. We'll all be here a year from now. He may not."

I couldn't think of anything to say to that, so we stood in silence on the dark football field, looking up together at the dark craters on the half-sliver of moon. Then, without a word, we started walking back up the field, away from the end zone, heading home.

Chapter Four

 Miss Merrill even looks pretty talking about slime molds.

She was standing in front of our third-period advanced biology class, summarizing the reproductive habits of the simplest forms of life. Afternoon sunlight streamed in from the window directly behind her, and I tried not to stare at the outlines of her arms and legs through her blue cotton dress as she ticked off the important points.

"The slime mold is usually classified with the fungi, but it's almost equally close to the protozoa." She raised her right hand for emphasis, and I saw that her arm was suntanned all the way down to her slender wrist. "During its motile phase, when it's found under logs and leaves, it takes the form of solitary amoebalike cells, or multinucleate blobs of protoplasm called plasmodia." Her soft lips wrapped themselves around the polysyllabic scientific terms with relish, as if she savored the feel of the long words. "During this motile phase, the slime mold feeds and grows."

She paused to brush her light brown hair back from her neck. She's a petite and naturally graceful woman — her slightest gesture looks like it belongs in a ballet. She's also the smartest, best educated, most independent woman I've ever met.

Miss Merrill finished all her premed requirements at Berkeley and could have gone straight to medical school, but she decided to take a few years off and teach high school science as a kind of public service. I think that's pretty commendable, especially since she ended up as my teacher. Today she was wearing gold hoop earings, and each time she swung her head toward the blackboard, the shining rings bounced beneath her delicate earlobes.

I listened and took careful notes, but another corner of my brain was far away, imagining the two of us on a cruise ship.

Lightning flashes across the sky, and mountainous waves wash over the deck and eventually capsize the boat. When the storm subsides, there are only two survivors: Miss Merrill and me. We're marooned on a narrow strip of South Sea sand, dotted with coconut palms and rimmed by pink coral reefs teeming with fish. She's not a science teacher anymore, and I'm not one of her students — we're both castaways in an underpopulated paradise. She's the only woman, and I'm the only man. We have to learn to depend on each other. . . .

"John?"

I blinked and realized that she had asked me a question. Everyone was staring at me, waiting for my answer. I forced my brain to work, recalling what she had just been saying about spore-producing capsules. "When the spores germinate, they produce amoebalike cells that become plasmodia all over

31

again, completing the cycle," I stammered, looking into her hazel eyes.

"That's right," she said, and glanced at her watch. "I guess that's enough for today. Tomorrow we'll look at the reproductive cycle of sponges." The bell sounded, and everyone got up and walked out of the room into the hallway. Miss Merrill gathered up her grade book and lecture notes and disappeared into the science department office, which connects to our classroom.

I hesitated a second at the wooden door, and then knocked twice, opened the door, and followed her. The science department office is large and windowless, and doubles as a storeroom for the chemistry, physics, and biology classes. Each of the three science teachers has a desk there, and the shelves that run floor to ceiling all around the room are piled high with everything from Bunsen burners to calipers to bird's nests.

I guess Miss Merrill hadn't heard me knock, because when I entered she was bent over her desk, putting away her notes. The top of her desk was covered with plant specimens she had collected herself: baneberry stems, with delicate white flowers; black oak-leaf clusters, with their tiny oblong acorns; and a fern I couldn't identify right away, with arching fronds and hairy rootstocks.

I advanced a few steps, but she still didn't look up. At the bottom of her light blue dress was a thin border of white lace that brushed her ankles. We were alone in the windowless office. I saw tiny blond hairs on those ankles, so fine they were almost invisible. Finally, I said, "Excuse me, Miss Merrill?"

Her head jerked up, and she jumped back in surprise. "Oh, John," she said with a smile, recovering. "You startled me."

"Didn't mean to."

"What's up? Do you have a question about something I said in class?"

"No. Not really."

She cocked her head to one side and asked, "Isn't there a track meet today?"

"Yup." I like the fact that she identifies me with the track team. It means she thinks about me in a context outside the classroom. "I'm gonna head right down in a second. Are you gonna come watch?"

"Can't today. I'm driving to San Francisco."

She seemed to go there very often. I wondered if she went to visit a boyfriend. "You must have a lot of friends from college who are still in the Bay Area," I ventured.

"A few. They scattered pretty fast after graduation."

I stood there with my hands in my pockets, feeling awkward and not knowing what to say next. The storeroom was like a scientific Chinese restaurant of mixed and exotic smells: There were all sorts of chemical odors and musty plant smells and rodent aromas from a half-dozen caged hamsters and white mice. "Is there something fun going on in San Francisco tonight?"

She seemed surprised by my question. "It's my parents' thirtieth anniversary. My sister and I are taking them out to an Italian restaurant. Why do you ask?"

"That's nice. No reason." I blanked for ten or fifteen seconds, and couldn't think of anything to say. I looked around at the shelves for inspiration.

"I found a strange butterfly chrysalis in the forest yesterday."

"What was strange about it?"

"I just never saw one like it before. It had unusual markings — white streaks like bird droppings for camouflage."

"Bring it in and we'll see if it's in one of my field guides." She began taking things out of her desk and tossing them into her handbag. I took a breath and stepped a little closer.

She was wearing lilac perfume. I reminded myself of what Glenn had said about just speaking the truth to women and not trying to figure out how they would react. But when I tried to speak, all I found myself saying was, "Do you think you've changed a lot since you were seventeen?"

She stopped loading up her handbag and gave me a quizzical look. "What do you mean?"

"Oh, I don't know," I said quickly. "I was just thinking about going to college and wondering if those four years will make me into a different person. I mean, how different do you think you are now from when you were in your last year or two of high school?"

She thought about it for a minute and laughed. "Very different. When you go away to college, you get exposed to all kinds of different things all at once. It changes you pretty quickly."

"What kinds of things?"

"New friends, brilliant professors, fascinating books, drugs, alcohol, sex, living away from home . . ." She stopped and smiled. One of the great things about Miss Merrill was that she would include drugs and alcohol and even sex on such a list without even hesitating. "And speaking of living away from home, I should be heading to San Francisco. Even as it is, I'll have a hard time beating the traffic. Did you have something you wanted to ask me, or did you just want to chat?"

"I guess I just wanted to chat," I said. "No, that's not true." I was about two feet away from her, looking right into those bright and friendly hazel eyes. "I wanted to ask you . . . to tell you . . ." My heart was thumping like it was going to jump out of my chest and do a tap dance on the tile floor. I stopped talking, and stood there with my mouth agape. I couldn't go forward and I couldn't switch into reverse; all I could do was stand there, stupidly inhaling that lilac perfume and watching her watch me. And then I suddenly began to cry.

She came over to me, concern making her face look even gentler than usual. "What is it?"

"I'm sorry. Something's wrong at my home. I don't want to bother you with it. I'm sorry."

"Don't be silly about bothering me," she said. "What kind of a problem is it? I bumped into your mother the other day in the supermarket, and she didn't mention that anything was wrong."

"It's not her," I said. "She wouldn't tell you. But . . . it's my father."

"What's the matter with him?"

I was amazed to feel a steady stream of tears trickle out of the corners of my eyes and slide down my cheeks. My body had started shaking a little bit, and when I whispered an answer, my voice trembled. "Leukemia."

"I'm so sorry," she whispered back. "Is it treatable?"

"Maybe." I was crying uncontrollably now, right in front of her. I hadn't cried this way in years. I had forgotten how much it hurts to let your feelings show this much. She walked up and put her arms around me and held me tightly. Tears burned their way down my chin and dropped off into space.

"I'm sorry," she whispered. "I don't know your father very well, but I like your family very much. Your mother is a wonderful woman. You must love him very much."

"No," I said. "I wish I did."

She let me go and looked at me. "What?"

"In some ways, I hate him. I think that's why I feel so bad."

She brushed my hair back from my forehead. "It's normal to have mixed-up feelings about your parents," she whispered. "I still do about mine. Look, I have to go now. But we'll talk about this again. And maybe you should talk to Mr. Cheeseborough."

He was the head of our guidance office, a bald, overweight man in his fifties who always seemed to be eating a snack. "No," I said.

"Okay," she said. "We'll talk again. Now will you do something for me?"

I nodded.

"Go wash up and get into that tracksuit and see if you can finish first today. I'm tired of seeing your name second in the school news."

Before I knew what I was doing, I reached up and kissed her on the cheek, and then I backed out of the room, fled through the biology classroom, and took off down the mostly empty hallway like I was in the final lap of a close race.

Chapter Five

A middle-distance runner without a kick is a very scared animal.

I've never been particularly fast in a straight-out sprint, and I don't think I ever will be. I've got endurance — I can run with pain as well as anyone. I can grind down most runners with perfectly planned laps that get quicker and quicker as the race winds down to a few final curves and straightaways. But if I hear footsteps going to the tape, in the back of my mind I always expect to be passed.

There were three of us now, way out in front of the pack. We were running in a tight little knot, so that six arms pumped and six feet rose and fell almost side by side on the cinder track. I led the way. Kellogg, my teammate, stayed just off my right shoulder. The other team's best runner, Dewitt, made a brave show of keeping up with us.

But we all knew he would fade. We all knew it would end up being between Kellogg and me. It always had been since freshman year, and before that way back to grade school gym classes. And no matter what I did or how early I opened up, Kellogg would win. He would stay just close enough to me to overtake me on the final lap. He would win because at birth God had given him a sprint kick, and for a middle-distance runner, a fast last lap is a glorious possession.

But not today. Today I was running on pure anger and frustration and love and embarrassment, all rolled into one tiny ball of energy. Today I had cried in front of Miss Merrill and then kissed her, and the mere thought of the encounter spurred me forward. I opened up with three full laps to go, and for a moment both Dewitt and Kellogg fell back in surprise.

There's nothing quite like taking the lead in a race and hearing the crowd roar for you. My rhythm felt great and my legs felt strong, and I even managed to move it up another notch as I passed the half-filled bleachers. Dewitt foolishly tried to stay with me. Kellogg fell back ten feet, and then fifteen, running just hard enough to stay within striking distance.

When people think about running, they always think about the legs and forget the arms. The pumping of the arms is what drives the engine. A lot of runners — particularly sprinters — work out with weights so that the strength of their upper bodies matches their powerful legs. With two laps to go, my elbows were rising and falling like twin pistons, lifting my knees and driving my thighs. Dewitt started to wilt. I could hear him gasping as his rhythm slowly fell apart.

With a lap and a half to go, Dewitt settled for third. His gasps became louder and louder, and suddenly he slowed and fell way back, and from then on I knew it was just Tom Kellogg and me. I was ahead by fifteen feet. Pumping and pushing and calling on every source of fury I could conjure up, I pushed it to twenty.

We reached the last lap. I heard the bell above the roar of the crowd, and glanced over my shoulder. Kellogg was still twenty feet back. He ran lightly and easily, his feet barely seeming to touch the track. He's taller than I am, with sandy hair and an easy, loping stride. Somehow he manages to run entire races with the hint of a slight smile twisting up the corners of his mouth. Not me — I grunt and grimace and suffer. The bell for the last lap faded into the distance and sank under the swell of applause, and I let it all hang out.

I know that football and wrestling are much more grueling sports than track, but there are realms of athletic torture that are reserved for runners — regions of sidesplitting, stomach cramping, muscle twisting, pure distilled pain and fatigue. The bell lap of middle-distance races leads straight through a particularly cruel domain. There's a moment toward the end of a close 1,500 meters when the sunlight dims and the applause fades and the other runners disappear and you're suddenly alone with yourself facing the eternal question: to slow or not to slow? Your breath is stinging and your stomach is knotting, and your brain is demanding: Why? WHY? *WHY?*

Why do this? What could be worth such agony? You don't have to stop, but why not just ease up for a second? Why not just slow the pace momentarily? And even as you try not to listen, your heart is thumping the same message

39

wildly, like a bass drummer gone mad, and you feel yourself run up against the barrier and start to slow. . . .

I hit the barrier with half a lap to go, and Kellogg closing. Maybe he was ten feet back; maybe seven. For a heartbeat I was alone with myself on that lonely threshold that every runner from Pheidippides to Roger Bannister has known and dreaded. I knew I had to pick up the pace to have any chance of holding him off, but to my horror I felt myself easing off on the throttle. Instead of running faster, I was barely keeping the pace. And suddenly, from just behind me, came footsteps that I recognized and hated.

We swept around the far turn and I saw the tape a hundred meters away, a thin ribbon of white stretching across the track and glinting in the sunlight. We ran by the bleachers and the crowd jumped to its feet, hooting and hollering for a new school record. Seventy meters to go. Somehow I clung to the lead. Fifty meters to go.

Maybe the last three laps had eaten up Kellogg's sprint kick and I would be able to hold him off. Thirty meters to go. My eyes were on the tape, ready to dive into it, as Kellogg drew even.

A middle-distance runner without a sprint kick is a scared animal, and now I knew that fear. Now I knew that no matter what heart and guts and effort I put into it, I would be shown up by that easy loping stride, and would watch the back of that sandy head of hair pull away to victory. For a determined, brave, reality-defying second, I ran even with him, my thumping desperate stride matching his effortless sprint.

Then there were six inches of daylight between us. Then a foot. And, then, as I dove for the tape,

I saw it stretch and break against his chest, and Tom Kellogg continued straight on with his loping, magical pace as I tumbled down into the cinders and rolled my way into my usual second-place finish.

It was a new season's best for Tom. Once again he would get his picture in the newspaper, and his name and winning time would be broadcast over the school intercom during homeroom. I waded through the crowd to shake his hand and congratulate him, and then I turned and walked off, ignoring teammates and well-wishers who tried to tell me how much they'd enjoyed the race.

"Great finish, Rodgers."

"Thought you had it this time."

"Hold your head up. You gave it all you had, John."

I beat the rest of the track team into the locker room and quickly showered and changed. Just as the first of them came in through the front, I slipped out through the back door and walked home alone. Maybe a few of them would wonder where I had gone, but none of them would dwell on it too long.

I walked home the long way, following the railroad track for a half-mile. It had been one of those days that you don't want to think about, but you can't help brooding about. Why hadn't I just told Miss Merrill simply and cleanly that I liked her as more than just a teacher? Why did I have to go and make an idiot out of myself, and embarrass both of us? And why, for once in my miserable life, hadn't I been able to pick up the pace on the bell lap and break the tape ahead of Kellogg? My father would have done it in his day, if he had run track. Glenn would have found a way to do it.

The railroad track stretched to the horizon in both directions, a steel pathway leading straight out of this dusty mill town. But instead of following the rails west toward Ukiah or east toward Colusa, I turned south onto Highlook Lane and headed for home.

Glenn and Katie and their spouses had left, so Dad, Mom, and I had dinner by ourselves, same as always. We dug our way through the first course of pink grapefruit halves without any conversation, and I started to hope that I might escape my father's usual dinnertime probing into my day. For once I just wasn't up to being polite. As we began sawing away at slabs of meat loaf covered with thick brown gravy, he turned to me and asked, "So, how was school?"

I felt myself wince. "Fine."

"Learn anything interesting?"

"No." Surely the tone of my voice would tell him to stop.

"Not even in biology class?" It's amazing how, when you don't want to talk about something, other people zero in on that particular area with uncanny accuracy.

"Nothing."

"Is something wrong?"

My mother sensed my mood. "Henry, maybe John doesn't feel like talking about school."

"If he doesn't, he can say so himself. You had a race today, didn't you?"

If there's one thing I've especially come to hate, it's my father's bringing up my losses in track meets. I don't think he actually has any interest in the sport — he just likes to hear about my failures. He asks his questions, and I have to describe my losing efforts across the same dinner table that my brothers sat at when they poured out tales of their victorious football and basketball and baseball exploits. I kept my mouth shut and studied the brown gravy on the side of my plate.

Dad waited about ten seconds for an answer, and then put down his fork. "I asked you a question. Didn't you hear it?"

I nodded.

"Then answer it. Did you have a race today?"

"You know I did."

"How did you do? Did you win?"

"Dad, please."

"Please, what? I just asked you if you won."

My hands were in my lap, clasped tightly together. "If you'd come watch me, you'd know how I did and you wouldn't have to ask."

His eyes narrowed a bit. "I worked this afternoon. And track is not a sport I understand."

"It's not hard to figure out," I told him. "They shoot a gun to start the race. The first person to break the tape wins. The second person finishes second. Lots of guys lose." We were looking at each other across our meat loaf. My mother was looking from one of us to the other, as if she were watching a tennis match. "You managed to come and watch my brothers play football. I don't think you ever missed a single home game."

"Don't push me, John. Your brothers played on weekends. You know I work during the week."

"You won't be working soon." I couldn't believe I'd said it, even though I knew I had. "So come and watch."

Dad's lip quivered. "You're excused from the table," he told me in a low voice.

"Henry," my mother said. Just his name.

"No," I told her. "It's okay. Thanks for a good dinner." I turned to my father. "I finished second again today. I lost. Does that make you feel good?"

"That's enough, John."

"Who says it's enough?"

"Go to your room and do your homework."

"I already did my homework. And why should I let you tell me what to do?"

He half stood out of his chair. "Don't push me, John."

"Then how come you get to push me?" I asked him. I turned, and walked out of the room and up the stairs.

I locked my door and lay on my back on the top of my bed, staring up at the ceiling. There were tiny cracks in the white plaster, fanning out in a circular pattern like a spiderweb. I began counting the cracks one by one. When I got up to twenty-nine, my eyes were distracted by some movement in a corner of my room. I glanced over, and then jumped up and hurried over to my terrarium.

The butterfly had hatched. The remains of the chrysalis dangled from the twig, its side split open in a gaping hole. Standing on the floor of the terrarium, looking back up at me inquisitively through its compound eyes, was a gorgeous blue butterfly unlike any I had ever seen before. My anger at my father and my confused feelings over what had happened at dinner melted away as I looked down at the newly hatched insect. I grabbed a pad of paper and two field guides, and sat down to try to identify it.

I've met lots of people like my father and my brother, Glenn, who have no interest at all in natural history. I bet my father's never looked at a bird or an insect in his life and wondered what order and family it belongs to, not to mention what genus and species. And I'm sure Glenn never wonders about how birds find their way south for the winter and then know enough to return across thousands of miles, or how a certain species of fragile insect survives our months of freezing cold. I guess there's nothing wrong with not asking too many questions. I know my father loves hunting and fishing — maybe you can enjoy nature more if you don't probe too deeply into its mysteries.

For me, the minute I see a new kind of animal or plant, or particularly an insect, I want to know all about it. And the best place to start is to identify it according to order, family, genus, and species. Maybe I get this curiosity from my mom — she doesn't study field guides or read naturalist magazines, but to sketch wildlife so accurately she must observe it closely and ask a lot of questions. In any case, as soon as I sat down with the pad, all my family problems were forgotten, and I was alone with a bright blue insect.

The order is easy. All butterflies and moths belong to the order Lepidoptera. I love the long and gentle-sounding word. One of my field guides explains that it comes from two Greek words: *lepis* for scale, and *pteron* for wing. All butterflies and moths without exception have scales on their wings.

After briefly consulting the field guides, I wrote down "Family: Lycaenidae" on the piece of paper. The Lycaenidae are a large family of butterflies encompassing the coppers, blues, hairstreaks, and elfins. What I had in my terrarium was clearly some kind of blue.

But what kind? I picked up the terrarium and studied the hind wings from underneath. The fringes were white, and along the outer margin were tiny orange crescents dotted with bright silvery scales. I glanced from the butterfly to the field guides and back several times, and then wrote down "Genus: *Plebejus*." The white wing fringes and the orange crescents made it a *Plebejus* without too much doubt.

But then I got stumped. And I mean really stumped. Because there are only eight species of *Plebejus* that occur in the Pacific Northwest, and I had pictures of all eight of them. I held the terrarium up and peered at the insect through a magnifying glass, studying the patterns of the hind wing markings. It clearly wasn't an Orange-Bordered Blue or a Northern Blue or an Acmon Blue. It was large enough to be a Lupine Blue, but the pattern of orange crescents made that impossible. I knew I could rule out the Arctic Blue since I wasn't anywhere near a tundra, and it didn't have the tiny black spots ringed with white of the Common Western Blue.

That left two possibilities. It was either a Shasta Blue or a Greenish Blue. According to my field guides, Shasta Blues are only found above the treeline on the highest peaks of southern Oregon and central Idaho. The orange crescents on their wings are supposed to be so tiny that it's difficult to see them with the naked eye. But the orange crescents on my blue butterfly were plainly visible.

So by the process of elimination, there was only one thing it could be. I wrote down "Species: Greenish Blue" on my pad. It felt good to have finally identified the little sucker. The only problem was that according to my books, both the male and female Greenish Blues have a conspicuous black spot near the leading margin of their forewings. I held the terrarium up to the light and looked and looked, but there was nothing on the forewings of my butterfly remotely resembling a conspicuous black spot.

So it wasn't a Greenish Blue. Except that it had to be a Greenish Blue.

I checked and rechecked the books, and studied the lovely insect from every angle. Its antennae quivered as I turned the terrarium from side to side, and its six tiny legs spread wide on the glass floor for balance. I wondered if it was trying to identify me in just the same way I was trying to identify it. The more the butterfly and I stared at each other, the more I felt a growing certainty that something was not quite right. I didn't know exactly what was bothering me, but something about the little blue *Plebejus* just didn't make sense. Finally I decided just to go to sleep and worry about it the next morning.

For a long time I lay in bed, facing toward the window so that I could see the night sky through the thin white curtain. The gibbous moon was a half-furled sail, plowing across the Milky Way. The clock on my bedside table ticked off the seconds, and once I heard the door to my parents' bedroom creak open.

I thought about the way my father had ordered

me up to my room in the middle of dinner. It easily could have escalated into a physical conflict. When he had half stood out of his chair, his eyes had been alive with both anger and hurt. If he had tried to hit me, would I have hit him back? The ticking of my clock seemed unnaturally loud. I tried to see the situation through my father's eyes.

What would it feel like to be strong and healthy, yet to know that a sickness is steadily eating away inside of you? Lying there in the blackness, I realized that I could not hope even to begin to understand his fear. Was it the prospect of pain that scared him? *Cancer* is a word like *torture* or *warfare* — it packs the promise of unimaginable misery into two short syllables. Was it the fear of death? Did the idea of simply ceasing to be seem so awfully frightening? Or was he afraid of the unknown, and of what might be waiting for him after death?

My hands clasped each other across my chest. I thought of the small graveyard plot my parents had purchased a few years ago in a cemetery in a nearby town. It was the only vacant real estate we owned — so far it was merely mud and rocks and turf. Would it soon be receiving its first tenant?

I found myself praying. Maybe this sounds strange, but I pray fairly often. I don't go to any kind of church or belong to any organized religion, but I've been talking to God and asking him favors ever since I can remember. It's a very personal and secret relationship. I would never tell anyone at school or anyone in my family about it — I can imagine Glenn hooting at the notion of me being a good little boy and saying my bedtime prayers.

I almost always pray at night. I barely whisper

the words — if there really is a God, I figure he or she probably knows what I want to say. Sometimes I don't whisper any specific thing at all; I just think of a big problem bugging me that I need help with. And even though I never get a direct answer or an immediate solution, I find that the process of praying makes me feel better. It keeps me from feeling totally alone. And to be honest, deep down is the lingering hope that somewhere, somehow, someone is listening and may even decide to lend a helping hand.

Dear God. Please protect my mother and make my father well. If he must slip away, let me find a way to reach out to him while there is still time. Even if we have nothing at all in common, I want to touch him and hold him. Help me to control my temper when he ticks me off. Let me be a success in his eyes, if only just one time. Is that too much to ask? Dear God. Please hear my prayer.

I drifted into half sleep, thinking of my father and Miss Merrill and the Greenish Blue that was missing its spots. The whirl of images fluttered into softer and softer focus, and finally kaleidoscoped into the bright and effortless flux of dreams.

Chapter Six

When I woke up the next morning, I had the answer. This may sound trivial to you, but big revelations sometimes come in small packages. *The blue butterfly in my terrarium had miniature hooks on its wings, to link its fore wings to its hind wings.* I didn't even need to look at it to know that I was right.

I lay there with the morning light casting a white rectangle across my bedspread, and pondered the significance of the discovery. I may not know much about how to romance girls or how to win 1,500-meter races, or even how to deal with my own father, but there is one thing I do know: *Butterflies do not have miniature bristly hooks on their wings.*

Moths do. Butterflies don't. It's one way of telling them apart. Except that my insect was undeniably a butterfly and it undeniably had the kind of tiny hooking device called a frenulum that moths use to link their fore wings to their hind wings while they are in flight.

During breakfast I ached to tell my parents about

my discovery, but I kept silent. Partly, I guess, I didn't tell them because I suspected that my father would think I was just getting excited over nothing. He might not openly ridicule me, but the look in his eye and the smile on his face would ask: "Who gives a damn if a butterfly has tiny hooks on its wings or doesn't have tiny hooks?"

The other reason why I kept silent was that my father might believe me, and draw some conclusions about the consequences of such a discovery. He's worked in the mill all his life. The idea that I potentially might be stirring up trouble by finding a rare or endangered species in the company's forest probably wouldn't occur to him, but I couldn't take the chance. If he thought that, even for a minute, I knew he'd react angrily and probably violently. He'd make me get the butterfly and let it go, and force me to promise not ever to mention it again.

So I ate in silence. And so did he. As I think I mentioned before, my mother's never been a big talker, so the three of us got through our bowls of cereal without ever saying a word. I don't think I'd ever felt quite so alone in my own family. I was practically brimming over with the desire to tell someone what I had found, but instead I finished the last few Cornflakes and carried my bowl to the sink.

I brought the terrarium to school, cradling it with both arms as I walked onto the school grounds so that I drew strange looks from everyone around me. I didn't mind the looks so much — most of the students at Kiowa High School already think I'm pretty strange.

Miss Merrill was taking attendance when I burst

into her senior homeroom class. All the guys and girls stared as I walked right up to the front of the room and plopped my terrarium down on her oak desktop. She looked up from her book, and for a second there was mutual awkwardness as we both remembered the last time we were together.

"What have you got in there?" some loudmouth in the back of the class wanted to know.

"It's a bug. Don't bring it in our room," a girl shouted. "It might get out of its cage."

"It's just a stupid butterfly," a guy in the front row reassured her.

I disregarded all of them and spoke quietly to Miss Merrill. "I need to talk to you."

"Now?" she asked.

I nodded.

"Can't it wait till after homeroom?" She read the eagerness in my face. "Mary." A tall girl stood up. "You're in charge of this homeroom today. Make sure everyone stays inside and keeps quiet till the bell rings." She turned to me. "Let's go."

We left the class and walked out into the empty corridor. She headed for the science teachers' room, and I followed her. "I'm sorry if I embarrassed you the other day," I told her.

"You didn't."

"Thanks for listening."

"You don't have to thank me."

"Did your parents have a nice thirtieth anniversary?" She looked surprised by the personal question. "I mean, did you find a nice restaurant and have a good meal and everything?"

"Sure," she said. "We had a great time."

We were alone in the long corridor, heading for the science teachers' room. "I like you a lot," I told her.

"You're one of my favorite students, even if you finished second again in the 1,500 meters." We turned into an empty science lab classroom and walked through it into the teachers' room. She flicked on the light, and once again we were alone with only specimens and scientific apparatus for company. "Now, let's talk. How's your father?"

"Fine, thanks."

"Are the two of you getting along better?"

"No."

"That's too bad."

"No, it's normal."

There was a silent beat during which she looked at me quizzically and I shrugged. "Isn't that what you wanted to talk about?"

"No."

"Then what?"

"Something that doesn't make any sense."

"What?"

"It has a frenulum."

Her eyes widened. "What has a what?"

I glanced down. The butterfly was standing in a corner of the terrarium with its blue wings spread wide. Miss Merrill followed my stare, and then we looked up at the same time and our eyes met.

"You mean this thing has hooks on its wings?"

"This thing is an order Lepidoptera, family Lycaenidae, genus *Plebejus*, species Greenish Blue. Except that it's not."

Miss Merrill looked confused, which I guess was

understandable. She gave me the tiny smile people flash at the completely insane. "Slow down," she requested. "You found this, right?"

"Yeah. I mean yes. In the company forest, a few days ago."

"And you identified it?"

"I tried to. Except that it doesn't have a black spot where it should, and it has hooks on its wings."

"Which doesn't make any sense because we both know that butterflies don't have hooks on their wings. So you must be mistaken."

I picked up a magnifying glass that was lying on a nearby table and handed it to her. She took it from me and bent over the terrarium for a long, long time. As she studied the butterfly from different angles, my eyes followed the shiny red curve of ribbon that tied her brown hair in a single lovely braid. When she finally straightened up, her face was tense with excitement in a way that I had never seen before. "John," she said, looking into my eyes.

"Yes, Miss Merrill?"

"This butterfly has hooks on its wings."

There was complete silence inside the little windowless room. We both looked down at the blue butterfly, which uncoiled its wiry proboscis a bit and then retracted it, as if showing off in its own small way. "I know," I said.

"I know you know."

We both broke into goofy, excited smiles at the same time. "So what do we do?" I asked her.

She thought for a minute. "Hammond Eggleson," she finally said.

It was my turn to be confused. "Is that a kind of omelet?"

A delightful little laugh rolled out from between her even, pearly, perfect rows of teeth. "Dr. Hammond Eggleson. He's a world-class entomologist I studied with at Berkeley. I'm sure there's a simple explanation for this, and he'll know what it is. Let me keep this butterfly in the lab till I talk to him."

"Will you let me know what he says?"

"Of course," she promised. "As soon as I find out. Now, we both better get to our first-period classes."

I spent that day watching the doorway of each of my classes, waiting for Miss Merrill or a messenger from her to come and get me. What would Eggleson say? It was too much to believe that I had really discovered anything important enough to interest a world-class entomologist. No doubt Eggleson would listen to Miss Merrill's description over the phone and puff on his pipe or whatever he smoked, and clear up this mystery by explaining exactly what I had forgotten to look for or had not found in my field guides. Probably I had struck the entomological equivalent of fool's gold — it looked rare and valuable, but it was actually nothing special. Even so, I spent that day watching the doorways of my classrooms and waiting for a messenger.

An office monitor came to get me out of sixth-period French. We were taking a pop quiz, and the rest of the class watched enviously as I got my books together and followed the monitor out of the classroom. I was confused by the direction she took. "Aren't we going to the science room?"

"No," she said. "To the office."

"But . . . didn't Miss Merrill send for me?"

"No."

"Then who?"

"Your mother called. She wants you to call her back right away."

Suddenly all thoughts of butterflies and Dr. Eggleson vanished. "Did she say what she wanted? Is there some kind of emergency?"

"I don't know."

"There must be for you to come and get me this way."

"I really don't know."

I sprinted the last few steps to the office where Mr. Nichols, the assistant principal, greeted me with a wave. "Good timing," he said. "Your mother's on the line right now. Here." He held out a phone receiver to me.

"Hi, Mom?"

"John?"

"What's wrong?"

"Oh, nothing serious. I'm sorry to pull you out of class. But I wanted to talk to you before we go."

"Go where?"

"Your father's doctor called this morning. He thinks your father should go to San Francisco as soon as possible for some tests. So we're leaving this afternoon."

"You and Dad?"

"Yes."

"Just for tests?"

"That's right."

"How long will you be gone for?"

"A few days, I think. Maybe not even that long. Will you be okay by yourself?"

"Sure," I said. "What kind of tests?"

"I don't know," my mother said. Her voice quivered. "Just medical tests. We'll call you from San Francisco. Are you sure you'll be all right at home? I could ask Mrs. Redding to let you stay with her family for a few days."

The last thing I wanted was to move into one of our neighbors' homes at a time like this.

"Don't worry about me. How's Dad?"

"He's outside, loading up the car. He wants to leave as soon as possible."

"How is he? I mean, how does he look?"

"Fine," she said. "It's just for tests. He'll be fine. I've got to go."

"Bye. Call me?"

"I will. I love you. Take care of yourself. Bye."

I hung up the phone. Mr. Nichols was hovering just out of earshot. As soon as I hung up the phone, he walked over and spoke in a soft whisper, which none of the secretaries could hear. "I gather your father isn't well?"

"Nope."

"I'm sorry. If there's anything I can do, I hope you'll let me know."

I was kind of surprised. I've never had much contact with Mr. Nichols, but he's known as a disciplinarian and a real mean guy. His reputation at our school is kind of like the local Attila the Hun. "Thanks," I said.

"I think the world of your father," he went on. "You know, we played on the same football team here."

"I didn't know that."

"Sure did. I was a junior — sat on the bench, mostly. But, boy, he could play. He used to drag three or four guys with him across the field. They'd hit him high and hit him low and wrap their arms around his legs, and still they couldn't bring him down."

"I should be getting back to my French exam," I mumbled.

He nodded. "Of course. Remember, if I can help in any way . . ."

"Sure," I nodded. "Thanks."

I sort of sleepwalked through the rest of that day, worrying about what sort of news would come back from San Francisco. I didn't ask Miss Merrill if she'd had a chance to call her old professor, and she didn't volunteer any information till the very end of biology class. As we were all heading out the door, she called. "John, come back for a minute."

"What?"

"I talked to Dr. Eggleson."

"What did he say?"

"That we were wrong."

"It's a known phenomenon? Something they just left out of the field books?"

She shook her head. "No, he said we must be wrong in our description."

"But we're not."

"I told him that. He's driving over this afternoon."

"Here? A professor from Berkeley is driving all the way here?"

"He wants to see for himself."

"When is he coming?"

"Around five. I'm going to wait for him."

"I'll skip track practice and wait with you."

"No," she said. "Go to track practice. I'm sure he'll still be here when you finish."

"Okay," I agreed. "Y'know . . ." My eyes flicked

down to the blue butterfly and then back up. "I'm a little scared. I mean, if this really is some kind of important discovery . . . since I found it in the company forest . . . do you know what I mean?"

"I know exactly what you mean," she said. "But you haven't talked about this yet with anybody else?"

"No."

"Then let's wait and see what Dr. Eggleson says. There's no use worrying for nothing."

I raced through my twenty team practice laps a lot faster than usual, my mind churning with worries about my father, and hopes and fears about what Dr. Eggleson might say. On the one hand, I wanted to have discovered something significant. On the other hand, I had some sense of what might happen if, against all odds, my butterfly did turn out to be an important find.

The lumber industry has been barely limping along during the last decade or two. A lot of mills have shut down operations, and as soon as the mills close, the mill towns that they support quickly shut down also. Among other battles, lumber companies have had to contend with environmentalists who feel that too many old trees are being cut down, and legal challenges from the government and from private groups trying to protect endangered species.

Environmentalists and naturalists aren't very popular in towns like mine. They're called longhairs and a lot worse names, and organizations such as the Sierra Club and the Audubon Society, and more radical groups that spike trees and stage demonstrations to try to protect the environment, are seen as dangerous enemies.

Just to give you an idea how bad it is — two years

ago I subscribed to a magazine published by a prestigious naturalist organization. The mailman must've peeked around the brown paper wrapper — maybe he thought I was getting a porno magazine or something. When he saw what it was, he told some guys in the neighborhood what he was delivering to me every month. The guys beat me up pretty bad, and one of their fathers who worked at the mill told my father why they'd done it. Instead of siding with me, my dad flew into a rage and chased me out of our house and down the street. It took my mom two days to calm my father down enough for me to come back into our house. Needless to say, I called up and cancelled my subscription.

I didn't even take the time to shower or change back into street clothes after track practice. I jogged straight off the track into the school and sprinted down the corridor. The school was pretty empty — most of the lights were turned off except where the janitors were cleaning, but I saw that a light still gleamed in the science room.

I burst through the door without knocking. Miss Merrill was standing next to a tall, broad-shouldered Viking of a man who I guessed was Dr. Eggleson. In my own mind, I'd pictured him as a doddering old professor type, with white hair, thick glasses, and clothes that were twenty years out of date. Instead, he had neatly clipped blond hair and a bushy mustache, a barrel chest and shoulders like an NFL lineman, and he was wearing jeans and a short-sleeve shirt that showed enormous biceps and a forest of dark chest hair. Miss Merrill seemed captivated by what he was saying, and I took an immediate dislike to the big scientist from Berkeley.

"Hammond," Miss Merrill said, "this is John Rodgers."

"The one who found it?"

"Yes. And my best student."

The big man extended an enormous pawlike palm. "Well, it's a pleasure to meet my best student's best student."

I shook hands with him. He had a grip like a trash compactor. "Hi," I said. "Thanks for coming."

He sized me up with a quick glance and smiled. "How was track practice?"

I was surprised. "Okay."

"Distance runner?"

"Fifteen hundred meters. How did you know?"

"I spent a lot of time at track meets myself," he said vaguely.

"Shot-putter?"

"And javelin."

"Hammond was an all-American," Miss Merrill told me.

Great, I thought. An all-American world-class scientist with the body of Hulk Hogan. Terrific. Standing next to him in my track shorts and T-shirt, I felt like a munchkin in *The Wizard of Oz*. "So, what do you think of it?" I asked him.

"I'd rather not give you an opinion just yet."

"But we did describe it correctly?"

"Yes."

"And it has hooks on its wings?"

Dr. Eggleson nodded.

"Have you seen one like it before?"

"No," he admitted. "But that doesn't mean it's never been seen before."

"I thought you were the expert."

He looked at Miss Merrill and grinned, and she blushed. "I'm not a lepidopterist," he told me. "And as a general rule, I like to be cautious. Very often in entomology one finds what one thinks is an important discovery — even a new species — and one gets all excited. And then it turns out to be something that other people have known about and written about somewhere else for decades. So it's best to go slowly."

I wasn't satisfied with his answer. "But it has hooks on its wings. There are no butterflies with hooks on their wings. If there were, you would know about them."

"Ever hear of the Australian Blue Skipper?" he asked me.

"No."

"The male of the species has hooks on its wings."

"It does?"

"Uh-huh. Which doesn't make your find any less potentially exciting. Links between the early stages of butterfly and moth evolution are invaluable. But let's go slowly, shall we?"

"We shall. I mean, sure," I mumbled. "What's the next step?"

"Are you free now?"

"Sure."

"Can you take me to the spot where you found it?"

"Yeah. But . . . it's in the company forest."

"On private land?"

I nodded.

"It might be best if we could go take a quick look without anyone knowing that we were there. Do you know a back way in?"

"You mean where no one will see us?"

"Exactly."

"Sure. But we'll have to climb a fence."

"In the interests of science, I'm willing to embark on a little covert fence climbing," Dr. Eggleson said. "Anne, are you coming on this adventure?"

"I wouldn't miss it," Miss Merrill answered. "I have some jeans in the back room. Let me go change."

She headed off, and I stood alone with Dr. Eggleson. On the desk a few feet from us, the blue butterfly sat in his terrarium, perched on a twig. We looked at it, and then at each other. "By the by," Eggleson said, "you haven't mentioned this butterfly to anyone around here, have you?"

"No."

"That's good."

"But to tell you the truth, I am getting a little nervous. I mean, my father works in the mill. . . ."

Hammond Eggleson patted me reassuringly on the back. "Don't worry about a thing," he said. "As long as we're careful and quiet, there won't be any trouble."

Chapter
Seven

I felt a little bit like a spy. I know that sounds crazy since I had practically grown up roaming these woods, but this time it felt different. This time I actually felt scared as I climbed the fence way back behind Thompson's Creek where the sharp wires at the top have been bent backwards.

There were lots of easier ways to get into the company forest, but this was the most out-of-the-way entrance. I wanted to make sure we stayed far away from the mill and any of its employees and watchmen. Also, I have to admit I was kind of curious to see if Dr. Hammond Eggleson's world-class science background would help him get over a fifteen-foot fence gracefully. I was sort of hoping he would turn out to be a klutz at climbing.

Eggleson scrambled over the fence like a joyful gorilla. He used a few nearby branches to help heft himself to the top, swung his legs and hips over, hung down so that his enormous frame was stretched out full for a second, and then dropped lightly to the ground inside the fence. Miss Merrill came over after him, and her shirt got snagged by a wire at the top. I started to call out suggestions for how she could free herself, but almost before I could speak, Dr. Eggleson had climbed up, freed the snag, and helped her down.

We hurried through the ribbon of tall grass that rims the inside of the fence. Dr. Eggleson and Miss Merrill marched behind me quickly and silently; I sensed that they felt the same way I did about sneaking onto company land. In a few seconds we reached the jagged tree line and plunged into the relative safety of the thick forest.

The trail was only wide enough for two people to walk side by side. I led the way, and Miss Merrill and Dr. Eggleson trotted along behind. I was still in my tracksuit, and I had to keep reminding myself not to break into a full run. Instead, I slowed to a fast walk and turned back to them. "We're getting close. Everything okay?"

"Yes. How did you originally find the nesting site?" Dr. Eggleson asked, huffing and puffing slightly.

"What do you mean, 'how'?"

"I mean, by what scientific method? Were you investigating a particular type of food source flora, or did you follow a trail of animal or insect predation?"

"I used the 'falling fifteen feet onto a buckeye bush method,' " I told him.

He smiled. "I'm not familiar with that technique."

"I was chasing a Mustard White and not watching where I was going, and suddenly I fell ten or fifteen feet and landed on a bush. The chrysalises were all around me on the ground, except for a few that I landed on and squashed."

"I see," he said. "I hope we don't have to reenact every detail of your technique in order to locate the site again."

"I don't think that will be necessary," I told him. "I'm sure I can find it again." I swung by Thompson's Creek just because it's one of my favorite places in the whole world and I wanted Miss Merrill to see it. The late afternoon was overcast, and the amber light that broke through the trees and reflected off the falls had a grainy thickness, as if it had taken on some of the sweet mustiness of the surrounding old-growth forest.

Miss Merrill stopped at the edge of the creek and laughed delightedly. "Well, this is charming. What an absolutely lovely spot."

"You should see it just after the sun comes up," I told her. "I've been here some mornings when deer come down to drink — the big bucks breaking out of the tree cover first, and then the does and fawns following after them when they know it's safe. And I've seen big trout lying just off that bank with their bellies on those flat rocks that match the color of their scales as they scan the surface." I stopped talking. Miss Merrill and Dr. Eggleson were looking at me in a very peculiar way. "What?" I asked them.

"I told you," she said to Eggleson.

"Yes," he said. "I see."

"What are you two talking about?"

"Just that it wasn't completely a coincidence that you happened to fall onto that bush and find the butterfly," Dr. Eggleson said with a surprising tone of new respect. "Now, let's find that nesting site."

We left the creek behind and started cutting through the woods in the direction that I had chased the Mustard White. There was no trail, and I had no markers to go by, but I've spent a lot of time hiking through this forest and I've got a pretty good memory and sense of direction. I was able to get us close on my first try, and within about half an hour we found the declivity with the squashed buckeye bush and the butterfly chrysalises.

Except that they weren't all chrysalises now. About a third of the pupae had opened. Here and there in the narrow rocky valley, sitting on saw grass or fluttering between thistle stalks, were blue butterflies just like the one I had in my terrarium. It was a silent, private place — the domain of very delicate and lovely creatures.

We stood together for three or four minutes without speaking, watching light blue wings catch the late afternoon breeze as the butterflies flew back and forth like hundreds of tiny sailboats blown and becalmed on a secret bay. Suddenly, Dr. Eggleson muttered, "Well, so," and broke into action.

He took a camera from a small satchel and began snapping pictures of the butterflies and the valley from every angle. Next, he collected small samples of plants and bushes and even the soil, all the time making notes in a small black notebook. It was kind of fascinating to watch him — I followed along behind, trying to stay out of his way and understand exactly what he was looking for and what order of steps he followed.

Miss Merrill walked with us, at times helping Dr. Eggleson collect and catalogue specimens, and at times talking to me in a low voice. She looked great in jeans and a flannel shirt. When we had a free moment alone, I told her about my dad going to San Francisco Hospital for tests.

"It's good that he's going," she said. "They've got great facilities there. I'm sure he's getting the best of care."

"But why did he have to go so suddenly?"

"The sooner the better."

"You said you don't always get along with your own parents?"

She laughed and shook her head. "Who does?"

"Which one don't you get along with? Your mother or your dad?"

"Mostly my dad."

"Why not? Does he want you to stop teaching, settle down, and get married?"

She laughed even louder, so that Dr. Eggleson looked around at us. "No," she told me. "He wants me to stop teaching and start medical school."

"Really? I think that's great. I mean, to be encouraged like that."

"Sometimes it's terrific," she said. "And sometimes it's not so hot. Sometimes, even though I love him, I wish he'd just keep his big mouth shut and let me live my life."

I couldn't think of anything to say after that, so we just followed along behind Dr. Eggleson in silence. By the time he finished taking pictures and collecting specimens, it was starting to get dark. "John," he said, "it just occurred to me that your parents will probably be worrying why you haven't come home from school."

"Not today," I told him. "They're out of town."

I exchanged a glance with Miss Merrill. She understood that I didn't want to tell Eggleson about my family troubles, and didn't say anything. It made me strangely happy that we shared secrets from him. "Will you tell me something?" I requested as he carefully packed all of the specimens he had collected.

"What?"

"Now you've had a chance to see the blue butterflies in their habitat. Have you ever seen or heard of anything like them before? Anywhere in California?"

He twisted his thick mustache in his fingers and looked at me. "No," he finally admitted. His voice dropped down almost to a whisper. "Not in all of North America."

My voice dropped down also. "And if it checks out — I mean, if it's a new species? Then what?"

"One step at a time," he told me. "And the next step is to get out of this forest before it gets dark."

We walked back in complete silence, climbed the fence without incident, and were soon in Dr. Eggleson's jeep, heading back toward town. The winding road was empty and he drove very fast, barely slowing around curves, so that several times the tires screeched in protest. He popped in a CD, and classical music filled the car. Then, he seemed to think better of it, and switched off the CD. "John," he said, slowing. "You deserve a better answer than the one I gave you."

"You mean about it being a new species? I understand that you don't want to say till you're sure."

"No," he said. "I wasn't talking about that. I was talking about you."

"Me?"

"You said your father works for the mill?"

"Yes."

"And there's logging going on in that forest?"

"Well . . . sure. Not in the part we were in. Most of it now is on the south side. Nearer the mill."

"They're clear-cutting?"

"Maybe. I don't know exactly." I hesitated a long heartbeat. "Yes, they are."

I was surprised to feel Miss Merrill reach back and take my hand and give it a gentle squeeze.

"I don't want to try to sound profound or anything," Dr. Eggleson said, "but sometimes people get chosen at some point in their lives to do something larger than themselves. Like Columbus discovering America, or a quiet railway engineer named Einstein figuring out relativity, or Marie Curie experimenting with radium and polonium." He stopped, as if embarrassed by his own attempt at speech making. "I guess those examples are pretty ridiculous . . . because of the magnitude of the discoveries . . . and because Einstein, Curie, and Columbus had dedicated their lives to exploring. Then, again, you were out there with a butterfly net chasing something, weren't you?"

"Yes," I admitted, and a small shiver shook through my body. "A Mustard White." Miss Merrill was still holding my hand. I was surprised by how warm her palm felt, and by how small her fingers were.

"Well, I guess what I'm trying to say is that you may have found something rather significant. And if you did, things won't be the same. I don't think

70

there'll be any serious trouble, but logging in that part of the forest will have to stop."

"They'll never stop . . ." I began, but he cut me off.

"I know it must be scary. But there's no reason for you to worry. There's no reason to tell anyone. There's no reason for your name to get out. I understand that if it does, things might not be so friendly for you around here."

"You really understand that?" I asked him, letting go of Miss Merrill's hand and leaning forward.

"Absolutely," he said gravely. "Think of me as a friend you can trust. Now, with your permission, I'm going to take what I collected and the live specimen you found back with me to Berkeley and show some people. And we'll take things from there. Okay?"

"If you promise not to hurt him."

"Who?"

"My butterfly. Don't pin him or dissect him or anything."

"I just want to photograph it and show it around."

"Okay. Because then I'm going to take him back and let him go."

"I understand," he said, and I could tell from the tone of his voice that he did. "Now, how do we get to your house?"

I directed him, and soon we pulled up to the curb outside my completely dark, two-story house. "This is it," I told him. "Will you keep me informed? I mean, I'd sort of like to know what's happening."

"Sure," he promised. "Now that Anne and I have . . . renewed our friendship, I'll be talking to

71

her often. And she can tell you what's happening. Good-bye . . ." He grabbed my hand in his two massive paws and gave it a big shake. "By the way," he said, still shaking my hand. "Have you decided where you're going to college yet?"

"No," I said. "I'm just a junior."

"Well, you might consider Berkeley. In fact, not that you'll need my help, but I might even be of some slight use when it comes time to deal with the admissions process. If you decide you want to go."

"Thank you," I mumbled, and scrambled down out of the jeep. As I stood on the curb, watching the jeep's taillights recede into the darkness, I suppose I should have been thrilled by Dr. Eggleson's offer to help me get into a very wonderful college. But, to tell the truth, I was thinking about the two of them driving off together in the jeep. Would they have dinner together? Would she invite him to her apartment?

I remembered my long good-bye handshake with the world-famous entomologist — he had not been wearing a wedding ring.

Chapter Eight

I don't know if you've ever been in your house by yourself. Not just all alone in the sense that everyone's gone away for a little while, but all alone because of a life-changing crisis, so that it will be days or maybe even weeks before anyone comes back. And you feel deep down that your home and your life there will never totally go back to normal. As I headed up the walk, glancing at the empty driveway and up at the dark bedroom windows, I felt real strange. I unlocked the front door and listened for a second — the floorboards weren't creaking, and the wind wasn't swishing against the windows. Instead, all was still and completely silent.

It was what they call *dead silent*. I'm not usually afraid of the dark or of being alone, but I felt a twinge of fear as I entered the dark house.

I locked the door behind me and walked through the living room to the kitchen, turning on lights as I went. In the kitchen I switched on the radio and started making myself a ham sandwich. I spread mayo and mustard on slices of rye, piled on lettuce

73

and ham, and stuck in an occasional slice or two of cheddar cheese. When the sandwich was about two inches thick and starting to lean to one side like the Tower of Pisa, I cut it diagonally, popped it onto a plate, took a root beer out of the fridge, and carried the makeshift dinner over to the television.

I've heard that some old people who live alone leave their TV's on all day for company. I never really understood how that could help them feel better, but when I clicked our TV on and a network newscaster's smiling face appeared on the screen, I felt relieved to have another human presence in the room. I wolfed down the ham sandwich and guzzled the root beer, and the sports news had just come on when our phone rang. I knew who it was even before I picked up the receiver. "Mom?"

"How are you?"

"Fine."

"Did you cook yourself dinner?"

"I just finished eating it."

"What did you make?"

I glanced down at the remains of the ham sandwich. "A very balanced and nutritious meal. Don't worry about me. Where are you calling from?"

"The Bay View Hotel in San Francisco."

"Is Pop there?"

"No. He's at the hospital. I'm going to go join him in a few minutes. I just wanted to make sure that you were doing okay."

"I'm the last one you should be worrying about now."

I don't think she believed me, because she asked, "Did you cook a vegetable with dinner?"

"Sure. A big bunch of broccoli."

"Why don't I believe that?"

"Mom," I said, "please don't worry about me. What's happening at the hospital?"

"They're still running tests. Depending on how those tests come out, they may want to start some kind of treatment right away."

"What kind of treatment?"

"I don't know," she said, and her voice sank to a fragile whisper. "Maybe chemotherapy, or . . . something else. I don't know. Right now they're just testing. . . ."

For a minute we were both silent, as faint static crackled over the line. "How's he taking it?"

"Great. He's doing great."

"And how are you holding up?"

"I should get back and see him now."

"Will you promise to stop worrying about me?"

"No," she said. "Worrying about you is what I do to cheer up. Bye, John."

She hung up, and I stood for a few seconds with the receiver in my hand. I realized that I hadn't asked if there was a phone number I could call at the hospital to talk to Dad directly. For some reason, that made me feel very bad. Not that I didn't have the number, but that I hadn't thought to ask for it.

I tried to do some trigonometry, but math has always been my weak spot and I can barely bring myself to do trig problems even when I have total peace of mind. So I ended up sort of roaming through our empty house from room to room, looking at things that I hadn't looked at for a long time.

The family trophy case is in a corner of the living room, near the TV. The four shelves are lined with dozens of different kinds of athletic mementoes: the enormous silver cup marked BEST ATHLETE IN THE SCHOOL, which my father got as a senior, my brothers' football and baseball and basketball trophies, and plaques my sisters had gotten for softball and cheerleading. On the bottom shelf, looking like tiny ferns in an otherwise impressive floral bouquet, were the three ribbons I had won in county track tournaments.

I was contemplating those three pathetic ribbons when I realized that one member of my family wasn't represented in that trophy case at all. It seemed strange, but it had never really occurred to me before that my mother — who dusted the mementoes in the case every week or two — didn't have anything at all on the four shelves. No trophies. No plaques. Nothing.

The closest thing my mom had to a trophy in the family case was one of her paintings, which hung on the wall opposite the TV. It was an oil painting of a winter scene — leafless trees and a frozen pond — done in muted colors. I must have looked at it hundreds of times before, but until this night I had mostly appreciated it for the incredible detail of the rendering. Mom had caught the wind-warped curves of the leafless limbs, blown in the same direction as the snowdrifts that blanketed the icy surface of the lake.

On this night, as I studied the painting, I wondered about the mood that had inspired her to choose such a bleak scene. It was lovely, but it was also about as lifeless as a picture of trees and a lake can get. Had she been sad or depressed when she started painting it? It was hard to think of my mother as sad or depressed. Raising five kids, she always seemed too busy to have any feelings of her own.

I thought back and couldn't remember Mom complaining or sulking or lashing out at us with a single explosion of bad temper. My father had been the volcano in the family, while my mother had hovered gently in the background, cooking dinners and applying Band-Aids and keeping everything running smoothly. Not to be cruel about it, but it was almost as if she didn't have any personality of her own. I looked up at the winter scene on the wall and shivered.

Our family photo albums are on a shelf above the fireplace. They're in chronological order, starting with the most recent ones, which are mostly filled with pictures of my brothers' and sisters' weddings. After those are their graduation photos. I had to dig back through three or four albums before I began to find pictures of real family life.

I spent an hour or so looking at the pictures from my early childhood, when my brothers and sisters were teenagers and we were all together in one big, generally happy and perpetually hectic family. There was a photo of my brother Nick and my sister Lynn, the two clowns of the family, trying to balance on my first two-wheeler. I'm standing in the background watching, fascinated and scared. I don't remember whether I was afraid that they would fall off and hurt themselves, or if I was scared that they might break my bike, but the terror on my seven-year-old features is unmistakable.

Another picture, for some reason, grabbed my interest — a snapshot of Glenn, my father, and me white-water rafting on the Rogue River. It's funny, but thinking back, I can only remember bits and pieces of that summer trip. It must have happened, though, because the little boy in the picture is unmistakably me. And he — I mean, I — look absolutely paralyzed with fear. I'm strapped into a life jacket that's much too big for me, and I'm holding on to the boat's rubber strap-handle with both hands. Wielding oars on either side of me, Dad and Glenn have big smiles.

I popped that album back onto the shelf. Looking at those pictures from my childhood, it almost seemed like a child from a different family had somehow infiltrated the Rodgers' household. I wondered, and not for the first time, if I had been secretly adopted or switched at birth in the hospital by mistake, or if my mother had been having an affair so that I wasn't really my father's son.

All of them would have seemed like plausible scenarios if it weren't for the fact that according to family legend, I had been birthed at home with the help of a midwife. There was a picture in one of the albums of me at age six hours, a fat, naked pink blob of a newborn baby squalling and clawing at the bearskin rug near our fireplace. As for my mother having an affair, she's just not the kind of woman who could do that. It would be easier for me to imagine my father dancing ballet.

The strangest thing about our family photo albums is the earliest volume from my father's childhood. There are whole albums devoted to my mother's family and her early years growing up in the nearby town of Kean. Her parents were fairly well-to-do, and there are pictures of her standing next to a big house with white pillars and a screened porch, and posing with her sisters and brother and my grandparents.

But there are no early photographs of my father. No baby pictures. No infant shots of him in diapers. No photographs of him romping around as a child. The first picture of Dad that I've ever seen is one of him in Kiowa Junior High School posing with the football team. He's the smallest kid in the photo by half a head, and his young face has an angry look. His black eyes are smoldering, as if he had to fight someone in order to get into the photograph.

I don't know anything about my grandparents on my father's side. Dad never talks about them, and for some reason none of us ever ask him. I know he went to junior high school and high school in our town, and lived with my uncle Mack and my aunt Lorna, who moved away to Toronto before I was born. But I don't have the slightest idea what my father's life was like before that, or why he wasn't living with his own parents.

Strange. Very strange. I looked at the angry face in that first photograph of my father as a junior high school football player one last time. Whatever he had fought through, the coal-black eyes in the handsome young face positively blazed. Was it rage at an unhappy childhood that had struck the spark? Fury at parents who for some reason hadn't been there for him? Heat generated by the friction of having to fight everyone and everything he came across? And how much did the unmistakable pain in those young eyes excuse serious faults in the adult man?

I sat there with the album on my lap and admitted to myself that I felt very guilty. My father was in a life-or-death situation, and instead of insisting that I stay by his side, or at least worrying myself sick about his illness from afar, I felt only a slight alarm coupled with curiosity at how things would turn out. Thinking about him, and remembering all his bullying of me over the years, *I could even feel anger at him at such a moment.*

But I couldn't seem to feel love for him. Sitting in the dark house, I wanted to very badly. I searched inside myself, but whatever it was that I was looking for didn't seem to be there. What was love in such a situation, anyway? Was it an ingot like a nugget of gold glowing in a dark mineshaft? Would I know it if I came across it, and could I seize it in my hand and hold it up to the light? Was it years and years of living with the same person, crystallized suddenly into the fear of losing him forever? If love was only the fear of loss, wasn't that kind of a pathetic little thing to go by such a grand name? Surely a son's love for his father should be a great and ongoing passion — a thing it didn't take the presence of death to summon out of hiding.

Yet, even with death all around me in the dark house, crouching in the corner where my father liked to sit after dinner with his feet up on the ottoman while he read the sports news and the comics; grinning at me from the window ledge like a horrific jack-o'-lantern turned the wrong way; and sliding down the oak banister that my father had scraped and varnished last month with his strong, calloused hands, I couldn't find a trace of the golden love I sought. Not a bar. Not a glowing nugget. Not even a tiny speck of pure affection glinting in the darkness. Nothing. *Nada.*

After a while, I put the album back on the shelf and stood up. I checked to make sure that all the doors and windows were locked, turned off the lights, and climbed the steep stairs to my bedroom. I glanced at the spot where the terrarium had been, and wondered where my blue *Plebejus* was on this dark May night. I lay down in my bed, pulled the covers up to my chin, and waited for tiredness to overcome guilt and grant me release into oblivion.

Chapter Nine

There were three of us standing around the long-jump pit after practice, tracing lines in the sawdust with the toes of our track shoes. Clark "Rhino" Rhinegold, our team's hulking discus thrower, was explaining that if he could do any event in track and field, he would choose the high jump. Rhino is the closest thing I have to a friend on the team, which isn't very close — he's just a big, good-natured guy who's friendly toward everybody.

"If I was a high jumper, I wouldn't have to work out with weights all the time," Rhino explained. "And I wouldn't have to run endless laps like you distance guys, either. I'd just show up the day of the event, loosen up for a minute, and then launch myself. Imagine getting six or seven feet off the ground and floating through the air like a feather!"

"If you got six or seven feet off the ground, when you came back down you'd leave a crater," Gus Daly told him, beginning the idiotic back-and-forth banter the two of them were known for. They were best friends, and the way they constantly insulted each other without ever getting really mad was beyond me. They were both very popular, and I hung around them sometimes and tried to listen and learn.

Gus was a hurdler, and he had twisted his leg during practice, which I guess had put him in a sour mood. He was thin and sinewy; if he'd been a fish, he'd have been a carp or a catfish — one of the species that people catch and throw back because they're too bony to eat. "Anyway," he said to Rhino, "you've got this high-jump thing all wrong. Who cares about high jumpers?"

"I do," Rhino told him.

"You don't count. How many high jumpers have fan clubs and groupies and get their pictures in newspapers?"

"Probably lots of them."

"Probably none of them. No, there's only one thing to be, and that's a sprinter. A Jesse Owens or a Carl Lewis. The world's fastest human. If you're the world's fastest sprinter, you can go anywhere in the world and you're an instant sensation." He looked at Rhino. "Tell me a place where people wouldn't honor you? Name any part of the world where they don't hold races to find out who's the fastest?"

Rhino scrached his nose and thought about it. "The Amazon."

"What do you know about the Amazon?"

"It's in Brazil."

"So what if it's in Brazil?"

"You asked me what I knew about it. I know where it is."

"You're both wrong," I told them, surprising myself. Usually I just listen. They looked at me.

"There's an event that's better than high jumping or sprinting or anything else. The long jump."

"Are you kidding?" Gus Daly asked. "You think there's something wonderful about jumping into a dusty pit?"

"He's got a point," Rhino agreed. "Soaring high through the air has class, but jumping into a pit doesn't sound so hot. What makes you think long jumping's so special?"

"Something I once read." I hesitated. I didn't know why I was bringing this up. The three of us were alone by the pit in the center of the oval of track. "Maybe the greatest moment in all of sports history," I told them.

"Better than Don Larsen's perfect game?" Rhino asked. "Better than Babe Ruth calling his home run?"

"He didn't call it," Gus corrected him.

"What do you mean he didn't call it?"

"He was just waving the bat."

"That's ridiculous. Everyone knows he called it. He pointed at the fence and then hit it right over that spot on the next pitch."

"Pure coincidence."

Rhino sounded shocked. "It's part of American history. To say it never happened is un-American."

"Are you as dumb as you sound?"

"No. But you must be as ugly as you look."

"Anyway," I cut in, "whether he called it or not, what I'm thinking of was better. It happened in 1968. Either of you guys ever hear of Ralph Boston or Igor Ter-Ovanesyan?"

They shook their heads.

"They were the two long-jump world-record

84

holders back then. In '68 they both came to the Mexico City Olympics to duel for the Gold Medal and try to set a new world record. Except that another guy came, too. An American. He had barely qualified the day before, and he wasn't expected to finish with a medal, unless he got real lucky and stole the Bronze. So when he went out for his first jump in the finals, nobody was expecting him to do anything special."

"How do you know about all this stuff?" Gus asked.

" 'Cause he reads books about it, you moron," Rhino told him. "Now shut up. This is interesting."

"Who're you calling a moron?"

"Three guesses."

"At least I'm not a blimp."

"You wish you looked like me."

"Only on Halloween."

I waited till they were done. "Just imagine. It's your first jump in the Olympic finals. You stand there looking down the Mexico City Olympic Stadium runway, psyching yourself up, and then you start to run. At first you feel slow. But your approach is one hundred thirty feet long, and halfway down you're sprinting about as fast as any world-class sprinter, and the cheering crowd becomes a hum and a blur all around you. You see the takeoff board up ahead, and somehow you push it up even another notch till you're flying along."

They stopped raking the sawdust with their toes and looked at me. I felt myself staring at the long and narrow runway to our long-jump pit, tracing a sprint with my eyes as my voice started to sound excited. "About three or four strides from the bar, you know that something's happened. You've broken into a realm of speed where you don't belong — where no long jumper belongs — and you won't be able to hold form for the jump. No way. No one could hold form at this speed. You'll miss the bar and run right through the pit."

My eyes reached the bar and jumped skywards. Rhino and Gus followed my glance, as if for a second caught up in the same miracle I was imagining. "Then you're in the air. Not flopping high and right away falling back down like a high jumper, but skimming along above the ground. While you fly, your legs continue to stride in perfect form — one big step, two, three . . . you could go on forever."

"Really, three whole steps in the air?" Rhino asked. "It must feel strange to stay in the air that long."

"Don't worry about it," Gus told him. "You have as much chance of getting airborne as Yankee Stadium."

My voice dropped to a whisper as my eyes started to trace a descent back to the ground. "Three long strides. You already know that something strange has happened, because the human body has limits to how fast it can run and how far it can jump, and those limits are extended by half-inches and inches over decades of grueling competitions. Especially long-jump records. They go up inch by inch over decades."

I had them now. They were completely in the moment with me, back to a gray October afternoon in 1968 when the son of a Queens, New York, shoemaker went into orbit. "Ralph Boston and Igor Ter-Ovanesyan have managed to push the world long-jump mark to 27 feet 4¾ inches. And then you come down out of the pit. *You've literally jumped out of the long-jump pit.* They have to measure the jump with a tape, because the sliding rod that they've been using doesn't stretch that far."

The three of us looked toward the end of the long-jump pit, imagining them stretching the tape while everyone in the stadium waited. "The tape goes past twenty-seven feet. Past twenty-eight feet. No one in the history of the world has ever jumped twenty-eight feet before, but the tape goes past it. Past twenty-nine feet. To twenty-nine feet two and a half inches. You didn't break the world record by a mere half-inch or a lousy inch, but by more than twenty-one inches. ALMOST TWO FEET!

"An entire decade will pass with no jumper even starting to come close to your mark. Then another decade, during which they'll start to inch close to you. Finally, twenty-three years later — nearly a quarter of a century — with all the incredible advances in weight training and technique, someone will finally jump this far again. But even then, he'll only beat you by two inches. On that evening in Mexico, you beat the mark before you by almost two feet!"

Something caught in my throat, but I forced myself to go on. "So after you make that unbelievable jump, you sink down to your knees and look up at the sky and for one minute you don't have any problems or worries and you don't even care about how stupid it is to be born and grow old, get sick and die and what's the point — WHY NOT JUST GIVE UP? WHAT'S THE POINT? — you're above that and beyond that. Because you've just done

something that no one thought could ever be done —
something beyond the reach of human beings — and
for one moment there in the sun, you're . . . beyond
death."

I shut up then. My voice was quavering, and I
realized that I had gotten way out of control so I
locked my jaws together.

"Bob Beamon?" Gus finally asked in a near whisper.

"That's right. Bob Beamon."

"I've seen the tape of his jump. It was incredible."

"It must have been tough on those two other
guys," Rhino said. "The two former world cham-
pions who were right there."

"Boston and Ter-Ovanesyan didn't even want to
compete after they saw what Beamon had done," I
told him. "They said they were afraid they would
look pathetic."

"Damn," Gus said. "I guess shattering a world
record in the Olympics would be the ultimate. Catch
you guys later."

He limped away, and I was left standing there
with Rhino, who was looking at me strangely. "You
okay?" he finally asked.

"Sure. Whatta ya mean?"

"I heard something about your old man."

I raked my toes through the thick sawdust.

"I heard that he was sick."

"He'll be okay."

Rhino crossed his big arms over his prominent
stomach as if he were suddenly cold. "I heard it
was . . . cancer."

I knew that he was just trying to be friendly, but

I couldn't stop myself from lashing out. "That's kind of none of your business."

"Sorry." He turned to go.

"Wait. How'd you get from Bob Beamon to my father, anyway?"

"You did, not me. Anyway, forget it. I just wanted you to know that I hope things work out. Let's talk about something else."

It was an uncomfortable moment. I guess I'm good at creating uncomfortable moments. "Like what?"

"I don't know. Anything." He scratched his nose, and I could almost see him rack his brain for another topic. "I hear Michelle Santos doesn't wear underwear."

Michelle was tall and sexy, with long, long legs. I was intrigued, despite myself. "What does she wear?"

He lowered his voice to a conspiratorial whisper. "Nothing."

"Just her jeans?"

"That's what I hear."

"Who told you?"

He shrugged. "I just heard it. When you think about it, it's kinda kinky."

"If it's true." I couldn't stop myself from saying, "People say a lot of things that they shouldn't."

"Yeah," he grunted. "Well, I gotta be going."

"Listen, thanks for asking about my father. He's gone to San Francisco for tests. We'll know more soon."

"You were right. It was none of my business." Once again, Rhino looked eager to change the subject in just about any direction. His last choice of a topic had been so unexpected that I was curious what he would come up with this time. "Say," he finally said, "you hear about that meeting?"

"What meeting?"

"Next Monday. There's a big town meeting about a new kind of butterfly that some big shot scientist from Berkeley found in the forest."

For a minute I couldn't even speak. "What are you talking about? What meeting?"

"At the town hall. The scientist is gonna come and make some kind of proposal. And people from the mill will be there to stop him. Sounds like it could be a pretty hot scene. I figured since it was about a butterfly and nature and all, you'd probably know more than I do about it."

I shook my head. "It's all news to me."

"A bunch of us are going to go listen. Wanna come see them give the scientist hell?"

"I don't think so. Well, maybe."

"He better bring police protection is all that I can say. Guys from the mill'll probably massacre him."

"Probably," I said. "I gotta be getting home now. See you tomorrow." And I started off at a jog that soon became a sprint as I neared the school building.

Chapter
Ten

Miss Merrill wasn't in any of the science class-rooms, and it took me about fifteen minutes of running through the school before I found her talking to Mr. Nichols in the front office. They looked surprised when I sprinted past the secretary in my track outfit, sweaty and out of breath. "Have you heard . . ." I began to blurt out, but I didn't get to finish.

"Yes," Mr. Nichols said. "We have. We're very sorry."

For a moment, I was completely baffled. "You told him?" I asked Miss Merrill.

"No, your mother told me," Mr. Nichols said sympathetically. "And I took the liberty of telling Miss Merrill. At your mother's suggestion, of course. Your mother and I thought it might be easier to break the news to you with the help of a teacher who's also a friend. But I see your mother's already gotten in touch with you directly, so you don't need us after all. If you want to take some days off school, or if there's anything we can do. . . ."

I stood there, blinking, looking from one of them to the other. "Could I talk to Miss Merrill alone for a minute?" I finally asked Mr. Nichols.

"Sure. If there's anything I can do to help, let me know. Your father's a fighter from way back, and I know we all pray he'll fight through this. . . ."

Mr. Nichols walked away, and I looked at Miss Merrill. I was almost afraid to ask, but I forced myself to do it. "What was he talking about?"

"Then you don't know?"

"Don't know what?"

"Your mother called from San Francisco. From the hospital. She wasn't totally . . . lucid . . . so I can't give you all the details. . . ."

"What did she say?"

"Apparently the doctors ran a lot of tests on your father, and his cancer is much further advanced than they thought. So they're beginning some treatments right away."

"What kind of treatments?"

"I don't know." She looked down at the tips of her shoes. "Your mother mentioned chemotherapy."

"Is my dad dying?" The words tasted like ashes — they stuck to my tongue. The only sound was the ticking of the office clock above the doorway. I suddenly felt cold, in a way that has nothing at all to do with room temperature.

Miss Merrill put her hand on my shoulder. "I don't know more than I told you."

I backed up, and her hand fell away. "It's a last-ditch kind of thing, isn't it? Starting chemotherapy so suddenly must mean they're desperate? He's dying?"

I could see that she didn't know how to begin to

answer my question. "They're making huge strides in oncology every year. I know people who've been terribly sick with cancer and gone into complete remission. It sounds like your father's getting the very best of care. I'm not one of his doctors — that's all that I can tell you."

I nodded and exhaled a long stream of air. The room felt so cold that I shivered. I had to get outside, into the sunlight. "Thanks." I started for the door on unsteady legs. It felt like the joints of my knees had come partway unscrewed.

"John?" I swiveled back. "You okay?"

"Uh-huh." I swallowed.

"You don't look so good. Why don't you sit down?"

"No. Gotta go."

"What did you come running in here to tell me about?"

It took me a minute to even remember. I found that I could talk in short sentences. "There's going to be a meeting. Next Monday. In the town hall. I wanted to know if you'd heard about it."

"What kind of a meeting?"

"Public hearing. A scientist from Berkeley is going to be talking. About a new species of butterfly. That *he* found in the company forest." I felt nauseous and swallowed several times quickly.

The shocked look on her face quickly turned to disbelief. "Hammond hasn't said anything about that."

"I don't guess he would've. We'll find out what's going on on Monday, with everyone else. I gotta go. Bye."

"But . . . he should have told me."

93

"Both of us," I mumbled and ran ten feet to the nearest trash can, sank to my knees, and threw up right there in front of the secretary and Miss Merrill.

The school nurse was summoned, and she helped me down to her office in the basement. She was a sweet but incompetent gray-haired woman who delivered occasional health education lectures to gym classes and always looked incredibly nervous when she had to talk to us about sex. I always felt sorry for her, since she was obviously in the wrong profession. Coming down the stairs from the office, I was so dizzy that I had to lean on her for support.

She had me sit on a padded table and took my temperature and my pulse half a dozen times. Maybe taking vital signs was the full extent of her medical training. While she repeated these procedures, I recovered and looked around at shelves of medicine and tongue depressors and bandages. The air in the nurse's office smelled soapy and antiseptic, and the more I breathed it, the more I wanted to get out of there.

I've never particularly liked being examined by nurses or doctors, even if what they're checking is routine. It makes me feel nervous and even a little helpless. Suppose they find something? Hospitals make me especially uneasy — I know lots of people get better in them, but I also know that some people don't. Intensive care floors and wards for the terminally ill seem like hotels that people check into to die. I sat there on the padded table, watching her take my blood pressure and thinking of my father and what he must be going through. Maybe that was one reason I hadn't gone down to San Francisco — on some level, I just didn't want to see it.

"You seem fine now," the gray-haired nurse finally concluded, "but I should really talk to one of your parents. Wait here."

"No." I hopped off the table. "You said it yourself. I'm fine."

"It's our policy to call."

I explained to her that no one was home, and that my mother had enough worries as it was.

"But according to our school health release procedure, I have to notify her that you're ill. Is there a number I can reach her at in San Francisco?"

"NO!" I half shouted.

She backed up half a step. "Calm yourself."

"I'M CALM. I'm fine. Thank you for your help. I feel just terrific now. Bye."

She took a step sideways, as if to block the door. "I won't scare your mother but I really should call her."

"DON'T YOU DARE! DO YOU HEAR ME?" Just like with Rhino and Gus out by the long-jump pit, I wasn't completely in control. I managed to get my voice down a few notches. "Can I just please get out of here? I'm really okay."

She nodded and stepped back out of the way, looking surprised and scared. I hurried out into the hallway, still feeling a bit lightheaded but pretty darn sure that whatever was wrong with me would never be picked up by a stethoscope or a thermometer.

I no longer had complete control over my temper and my actions — I was turning into a real psycho.

Chapter
Eleven

The lightheadedness and nausea that I felt that day in the main office cleared up, but even so the next few days passed by in a sort of nervous and feverish blur. I shivered a lot, even though I wasn't cold, and I got stomachaches at the strangest times. Twice, stomach pains woke me up at night out of deep sleeps, and I found that I was drenched in sweat. My nervousness increased till I didn't really feel like eating anything, which was strange because normally I have a big appetite. I lived on occasional snacks: an apple here, a bag of potato chips there.

I talked to my mom several times and told her I wanted to take the bus to San Francisco, but she insisted that I should stay at home. She said she and my father were doing fine, and that it was calming for her to know that I was attending school and still leading a normal life. I never told her about my strange diet and my stomachaches.

Glenn and his wife Lisa drove to San Francisco and kept my mom company at the hotel for a few days, and they agreed that I should stay at home. In the one brief conversation I had with my father, he got angry that I even suggested coming to San Francisco. "Don't be stupid. What the heck good would you do here?" he demanded, sounding very much like his old self. "Everyone's making so much of a fuss. You just look after yourself."

I didn't know what to say or ask. "How are you feeling?"

"Crappy. How's the house?"

"Fine."

"Who's cooking your meals?"

"I'm making do."

"Scary thought. How's school?"

"Fine." It was the inquisition again, same as always, and even though he was questioning me from a hospital bed, I felt my anger begin to rise. "Mr. Nichols says hello."

"Who?"

"Mr. Nichols. Our assistant principal. He says he played football with you."

"Oh, yeah. That guy. He didn't play. Sat the bench mostly. 'Fraid to take a hit. You win any track meets?"

"No, sir, I haven't."

"Found a date for the prom yet?"

"I can't choose between all the girls that want to go with me."

"Yeah, right." There was a long pause. "I gotta go now. Here's your mother. Take care of yourself, huh." And as my mother came back on, I heard my father in the background begin to discuss the day's baseball scores with Glenn.

On Thursday, Miss Merrill took me aside in the

school cafeteria to ask me about my father and to tell me that she hadn't had any luck trying to contact Dr. Eggleson. "It's strange. He doesn't return my calls."

We were at a table by the window, all alone. Several tables down, a couple of freshmen were starting a food fight. They didn't seem to mind that Miss Merrill, a teacher, was nearby. Maybe they didn't know she was a teacher. In slacks and a red T-shirt, she looked young enough to be a high school senior. "I don't find that strange," I muttered.

"Why not?"

"It's about what I would have expected from him."

"What's that supposed to mean?" She sounded a little angry. "You don't think he's . . . trustworthy?"

"Apparently not."

"He was the best teacher I had at Berkeley. The best teacher I've ever had."

"That doesn't make him trustworthy."

"He's a wonderful man. I'm sure there's an explanation."

An empty milk carton from the food fight rolled across our table. I stopped it with my hand and slowly squashed it, and looked right into her bright hazel eyes. "He's decided to take over the show. Make it his butterfly and his issue."

"Hammond's not like that."

"We'll find out soon. Monday's only four days away."

Before she could answer, the food fight really got going, and a turkey drumstick sailed between us. Miss Merrill went over to quell the minor riot, and I walked away.

My feelings of nervousness grew worse and worse

until they seemed to twist together into a knot of pure, cold, unreasoning dread. By Saturday afternoon I found I couldn't sit still and study for more than ten minutes at a time, so I ended up going out for a long walk.

I thought it would calm me down to see people I knew, so I headed right for the center of town. The main intersection of Kiowa is at the corner of Grand and Mill. The Kiowa Pharmacy, a bank, the Mill Insurance Corporation, and the Good Guys Saloon face out from different directions toward the traffic light. I guess the fact that three of the four buildings are administered by the mill is a good indication of just how much the lumber mill nourishes and dominates every aspect of our town, and has done so since the turn of the last century.

The Good Guys Saloon was built in the 1940's completely of old-growth redwood. The facade has darkened a bit over the years, particularly around the edges — the old wood gives the tavern a soft, down-home kind of look. I doubt anyone could afford to build an entire building of old-growth redwood these days. Lumber from the giant old trees costs three or four times more than wood from younger redwoods.

I've heard it said that each of the great sequoias in the company forest is worth more than ten thousand dollars, and that the largest trees are worth almost double that. Imagine — a single tree worth twenty thousand dollars! I guess it's understandable that attempts to get lumber companies to stop harvesting the giant old trees often meet with violent resistance.

It was just a little past four, but I could tell that

the saloon was already crowded by the street traffic near the door. Hank Granger, all three hundred-odd pounds of him, was seated on the bouncer's stool at the door. He waved a huge arm at me as I passed by. "Heard 'bout your dad. Give him my best."

"Will do."

Peering through the window as I passed, I could see five or six sturdy men standing around a pool table watching a guy line up a shot. Behind them, a second row of spectators, mostly girls in their early twenties, sat at the bar. I knew everyone in the bar by name, and they knew me and my family. A couple of them saw me peering in and waved. I had thought that seeing familiar faces would calm me, but the friendly waves only seemed to make me more nervous.

Country-and-western music drifted out through the open door:

> *"He was rough and he was rowdy,*
> *He was mean and he was tall,*
> *But a man without the woman he loves*
> *ain't really a man a'tall."*

Beneath an American flag in the window, a sign proclaimed: WE SUPPORT THE TIMBER INDUSTRY. And, as a joke, there was a smaller sign reading: TODAY'S MENU: SPOTTED OWL OMELET. MARBLED MURRELET HASH.

The spotted owl and the marbled murrelet are perhaps the two most famous examples of species that have brought environmental groups and lumber companies into direct confrontation. Environmentalists claim the birds need to be protected even if that means halting cutting in some areas. Lumber companies say they're barely earning a profit as it is.

The people who live in mill towns like mine feel their livelihood threatened and don't take kindly to outsiders from San Francisco or Los Angeles coming in and chaining themselves to bulldozers, or driving spikes into trees so that saws will not be able to cut them. I've read about confrontations getting pretty ugly, but so far there have just been a handful of small incidents in my town. We've been lucky — the storm of controversy has passed us by.

I continued on down Grand, exchanging greetings with just about every person and family I passed. With each wave and greeting, the knot of dread in my stomach grew tighter. Kiowa is a small town, and everybody knows everybody else. That has its good side and its bad side. As long as you're on the inside — part of the community — even the roughest, hardest-drinking rednecks generally treat you pretty well. Because of my brothers and especially my father, people generally treated me with respect. But if you slip outside that charmed circle of small town goodwill, God help you.

People here grow up fast and tough. The mill is the major employer, and most of the jobs are the kind that put muscles on arms and calluses on hands. On Sunday a lot of well-dressed and well-behaved families make their way to church, but I've also seen fights on Main Street in broad daylight a lot meaner than anything I've ever seen faked on TV professional wrestling. Once I saw a guy get his ear bitten off. Another time two women went at it outside the Good Guys Saloon. They grabbed handfuls of each other's hair, and it took the police nearly half an hour to separate them.

I felt so nervous that I could hardly stand up, so I cut my walk short and headed home. The sun was sinking behind the church, supposedly the oldest building in our town. The Reverend Hathaway, a sprightly, balding man in his early forties, was sweeping the stone steps. He looked up as I passed and waved to me, and then put down his broom and walked out to greet me. "John, how's your dad?"

"Fine, thanks." I was a little surprised that the reverend would go out of his way to inquire about my father. Dad isn't exactly religious; I don't think he's ever been inside the old church in his entire life. He believes that religion is hogwash, and he brought up all my brothers and sisters as atheists.

I'm probably the only member of the family who believes in God at all, and I wouldn't exactly hold myself up as a model of faith. Sometimes I think I just *want* to believe that something else is out there somewhere, and that the fact that I pray to a divine being for help is really a combination of weakness and cowardice.

"Sure is lovely out," he said. "My favorite time of year."

"Couldn't be much nicer," I agreed, eager to get away. The late afternoon shadows were lengthening on the church lawn.

"Your father's a strong man. He'll pull through."

I nodded. "I gotta get home now."

"And I'd better get back to sweeping. . . . " He started toward the steps and then turned back, looking faintly embarrassed. He smiled and scratched his ear. "John, I know your parents aren't members of the church, but if you ever need someone to talk to . . . I know it's a hard time."

"Okay," I said, feeling a little bit embarrassed. "Bye."

"Bye."

I took the shortest route home, seeing the same houses that I had seen all my life, waving to the same people on the same porch rockers, stepping on the same cracked sidewalks, and inhaling smells from the same neatly pruned flower gardens. It certainly was a tight little community — tough, yet caring; boring, yet wholesome. I was struck by how little it had changed in all the years I had grown up. Like it or not, I was a part of this world.

So why did I feel so nervous? The knot in my stomach wound tighter and colder than ever. Surely it wasn't the town and all the familiar faces that were doing this to me?

I hated this place. I was looking forward to leaving it soon and going far away to college. It would be great to get out, to escape to a city. But in the back of my mind I had always felt certain that the town would go on in my absence the same way it had for the last hundred years; the mill would churn along, and my parents would still live here, and once in a while I would come back and visit for a few days.

Now, as I finished my walk and headed up to my house, I wasn't so sure. I thought of my dad in the San Francisco hospital. The town meeting about the butterfly was only two days away. Changes were looming on the horizon, and even though I hadn't been particularly happy in this little mill town of my childhood, it was kind of scary to think that Kiowa might never be the same again.

But that wasn't what *really* scared me. That wasn't what scared me so much that I could barely walk up the path and swing our front door shut behind me. It wasn't until late Sunday night that I figured it out. I was lying in bed, eyes open, looking at the moonlit rooftops of the houses near my own, when suddenly the truth came to me.

What was scaring me so much was a premonition that somehow I was destined to be the agent of destruction of this neat little world of my childhood. On my walk I had felt like a dangerous interloper — a spy embraced by the trusting; a wolf welcomed into the fold.

It was an awful feeling. Thrilling and terrifying.

I didn't know exactly how or why or what, but I sensed deep down in my guts that something momentous and irreversible was about to happen.

Chapter
Twelve

I decided to take Rhino up on his offer to go to the town meeting, so on Monday night I met him and a bunch of other guys from our school in the lot behind the Exxon station off Route 6. Gus Daly had gotten his older brother to buy beer. A half-dozen or so guys showed up, and for a long time we all stood around in a semicircle, drinking and talking and trying to stay warm.

A joint was passed around the semicircle, and I watched the tiny orange-red circle glow each time someone inhaled. When it was my turn, I waved to decline it, and then realized that I was supposed to pass it to the next guy whether I wanted to try it or not. Being around drugs of any kind makes me real nervous. I downed my first beer much too quickly, and someone handed me a second one. I could smell the marijuana, and I kept waiting for the drone of a police siren. The conversation that bounced back and forth around the semicircle seemed to get rougher as we finished second and then third beers.

It had grown pitch dark. Now and then a car sped

by on Route 6. The Exxon station had been closed and boarded up for more than six months, but a faint smell of gasoline lingered around it. I must have been a little drunk, because even though I knew everyone present, I began to have trouble identifying who was speaking. The anger in the voices that floated out of the darkness was impossible to miss.

"You know what I hear? This guy wants to close down the mill. And he can do it."

"No way in hell. It's a private company."

"Doesn't matter. My cousin up in Bridal Veil — had a job one day, out of work the next."

"So *if* this guy could *really* close it down, why bother with this meeting?"

"Rubbing our noses in it, probably."

"Yeah, these longhairs love to bust our chops."

"We'll see who busts who."

"Damn straight. I hear some of the guys'll be looking for him afterwards."

"Hope they find him."

"He isn't likely to stick around town."

"Not if he's smart."

"He's a professor."

"Doesn't mean he's smart. Some of the dumbest people I ever met were teachers."

"What'd this hotshot find that's so important, anyway?"

"Get ready for this. A bug."

"A bug? You're kidding, right? You sure he didn't pull it out of his own long hair?"

"This is a special bug. Some kind of mutant butterfly."

"Give me another beer. We're all out? Well, we should be heading over. You sure he wants to close down the mill for a butterfly? Why the hell are they even letting him speak?"

"Shouldn't let him out of town in one piece is all I can say."

"Maybe they won't."

We tossed the bag of empty bottles on top of a Dumpster that was already overflowing, and headed off to the town hall. The three beers drunk one after the other had had their effect, and I found myself stomping hard and awkwardly with each step, as if marching to an uneven beat. I was drunk and I was scared. Their talk of violence toward Dr. Eggleson had boomeranged my way in the darkness. Once again, I had the terribly uncomfortable feeling of being an enemy among people who treated me like a friend.

We reached Grand Street and were swept up in a stream of people moving toward the big town hall. There were a lot of men still in their uniforms from the mill, broad-shouldered loggers and plank cutters who walked together in angry little clusters. Their faces were hard and serious under the streetlights. I could see stubble on many chins; they had gotten up and shaved at sunrise, before setting out for work nearly fifteen hours ago.

I saw other guys and girls I knew from high school, a lot of them in Kiowa varsity jackets, their hands in the pockets of their jeans as they walked through the cold evening air. Families came with small children, the mothers anxiously keeping their three- and four-year-olds close like hens clucking at chicks. And then there were the old people who had braved many cold northern California winters, walking along with canes or arm-in-arm for support, some of them so frail and the lines in their faces chiseled so deeply that you could see the weakness and miss the pride if you didn't know them better.

The town hall was built a decade or so ago, just before the bottom fell out of the lumber industry. It's a lovely building — two great sequoia trunks rise as pillars in the center, connecting the polished wooden floor to the beamed roof overhead. I'd been to a couple of big town meetings there and also to a few concerts, but I'd never seen the hall full before. As we filed in through the big doors and fought our way to seats in the second row, the hall was filling up quickly. Already some young men had elected to stand on the sides, and give their seats to old people. Five town policemen and two firemen stood between the crowd and the platform, chatting among themselves.

A few of the most important men in our town stood on the stage. Mayor Stokes, looking dapper in a gray wool suit, kept running down the steps from the platform to shake hands and exchange opinions with friends. I guess for a politician, any public event is a chance to gain votes. Near the mayor I spotted Irv Cross, the tough old chief of police, talking to Stanley McKeon who took over running the mill from his father a few years ago. I wondered if they were discussing security — from what I had heard in the parking lot of the Exxon station, it sounded like things could get out of hand very quickly.

"John? John!" I looked down the front row and saw Miss Merrill standing and waving only fifteen feet away. I waved back and wished I were sitting with her. We shared a secret bond — we were the only two people in the crowd who knew the full story of how the butterfly had been found. She didn't look nervous at all. She was wearing tan slacks and a red turtleneck sweater, and was chatting with the parents of some of her students.

The lights flickered, and the clamor of conversation sank to a buzz. Then the lights dimmed, and there was silence. Mayor Stokes stood up and walked to the microphone. For some reason I didn't understand, there was a burst of applause, and the mayor let the clapping go on for fifteen seconds or so. I guess people were sort of showing support for our town. Finally, the mayor raised a hand for silence.

He was a short, trim, amiable little man of about fifty, with old-fashioned sideburns and a surprisingly deep voice. "There have been a lot of rumors flying around about exactly what is going on," he said. "Let me tell you what I know. A few days ago, I received a phone call from a professor at Berkeley. He said that something had been found in our company forest land that has important implications for our town. He said he didn't want to hurt business here, and he requested a meeting. I agreed at once, and suggested that the two of us meet privately, or that he could come and meet with some representatives of the mill. But he had something else in mind. He wanted a public forum. Well, now he's got one."

Mayor Stokes paused for a moment and looked out over the audience, as if calculating something from the faces he saw and from the depth of the silence in the large hall. Finally he nodded and said much more conversationally, "I'll tell you the truth, I don't like this one bit. But if this guy wants to talk to us badly enough to come down here all by himself, then I think we should hear him out. So here's what we're gonna do. First, he'll say whatever he has to say. Then, he'll answer your questions. And finally, some of us up here on the stage may wish to make some short closing comments. I'm going to ask Police Chief Cross to maintain strict order — anybody raising his voice . . . or throwing anything . . . or making any other kind of trouble, will be ejected. Okay, then. Professor . . ."

The mayor sat down, and for a long moment everyone in the hall seemed to hold their breath. Then Professor Eggleson calmly stepped out onto the stage from one of the wings and walked to the microphone. He was dressed casually in gray corduroy pants and a blue blazer, and he carried a plastic terrarium in his right hand. A ripple of surprise ran through the audience at Dr. Eggleson's youth and size. "Hi," he said. "I'm Hammond Eggleson." He leaned his elbows on the speaker's rostrum and grinned. "If you wanna throw something at me, I'm a big target — should be pretty hard to miss."

That cut the tension. There were chuckles and a few people clapped at his bravado. Even though I didn't like the guy, I was impressed. For an entomologist, he had a lot of stage presence and pretty damn steady nerves. I glanced over at Miss Merrill. She was sitting forward on her seat, her hands folded neatly in her lap, watching every move her esteemed professor made.

Eggleson lifted the plastic terrarium above the rostrum. "This is the little critter we're here to talk about. It's a butterfly — order Lepidoptera, family Lycaenidae, and genus *Plebejus*." Listening to him roll off the names I had discovered for myself in my room using field guides gave me a little thrill. Eggleson stopped at the genus. "And that's it," he said. "It doesn't have a species. Because this butterfly and his relatives in your forest are unique, at least as far as we know now. Never been seen before. They may not exist anywhere else. Which brings us to a very touchy pass. What do we do now?"

Eggleson shrugged his massive shoulders slightly, as if to show that he didn't know, either. He lowered the plastic terrarium back onto the speaker's rostrum, took the microphone out of its stand, and stepped forward to the edge of the platform so that he was looking directly down at us. He looked enormous up there, and the thoughtfulness in his face was evident under the bright lights.

"Well," he said, "since I'm a professor of entomology, you can probably guess where my loyalties lie. I like bugs. But I was born in a town not so very different from this one. I've seen the battles in the last decade or so — I've been in a couple of ugly ones myself — and I'd like to avoid one here. There has to be a better way.

"If I'd met with the mayor privately, I would've ended up meeting with the mill people later on. I have a pretty good idea what they would have said, and eventually you would have heard about the whole thing secondhand. So, since time is, as they say, of the essence, I thought I'd cut right through a few steps and meet with you all at once. It's really pretty simple. There are only two ways we can go."

I looked around me . . . everyone was watching him as if he held their fates in his big open right palm. My own hands were together in front of me, my fingers tightly clenched.

"First," he said, "we can go the usual route, which

is a pretty rocky road. I talk to legal advisors and environmental groups, and we try to get this butterfly declared a threatened or even an endangered species. We go to the state. Then the federal government. Possibly also to the courts for some kind of restraining order to stop you from cutting timber near its habitat. And while we're doing that, you're doing everything you can to delay us and stop us. Also, you speed up your logging and cut more old growth. Environmental groups come in and try to protect the trees. And the cops in this room and probably all the cops in this town won't be able to prevent bloodshed . . . that is, if they even want to prevent it at that point."

The casual mention of bloodshed struck a nerve in the crowded hall. It was clear that Dr. Eggleson knew what he was talking about, and that he had seen such a scenario played out before. It was also obvious that he was totally unafraid.

"Anyway," Eggleson said, "that's one path we can take. And I'll tell you right now that if we go that way, eventually you good people in this hall will be the losers. Because the government of the United States, in its wisdom, will eventually decide to protect this butterfly and close down your mill. You'll end up looking for work and a new place to live. But there is another way."

He stepped to the very edge of the stage, so that it looked like he might dive off at any moment. I could see his face clearly — he was only about thirty feet away. I don't think he could see me, though. He was looking fixedly at the center of the hall, and as he began to outline his second option, he put every ounce of persuasion into his voice.

"All across this country, whether it's the Golden-cheeked Warbler in Texas, the red squirrel of Arizona, the Colorado Squawfish, or the spotted owl that you've all heard so much about around here, the same questions we're facing tonight keep coming up. Do we develop and consume, or do we protect and save? I think it's just plain stupid to go on pretending that it has to be resolved one way or the other. Why can't we work together? I have no reason to want to put you guys out of business. And I think most of you probably have better things to do with your time than killing off a rare species.

"So, in a nutshell, what I'm proposing is this. I've consulted the top experts, and right now we don't know enough about this butterfly to even begin to guess what it will take to protect it. It seems to live in a very circumscribed habitat. There may be ways of protecting it that won't endanger your timbering operation. I want you to let us into your forest for a three-week study." There was an angry rumble from the crowd. Eggleson waited for the sound to die down. "We'll be quick and we'll be fair, and I can promise you that what we'll be looking for is a way to keep you in business and protect this butterfly. And after three weeks, well . . . we'll take it from there. But we'll try to work together. I'll be happy to answer any questions now."

David Mitchell stood up. He's a foreman at the mill, and one of the toughest men in Kiowa. I could see his muscles even under his thick red flannel hunting jacket. He looked up at Eggleson without much fondness, and I thought that if these two men ever came to blows, it would be a real battle of heavyweights. "I'm no scientist," he said. "I'm a plank cutter. I have a question about this bug you found. What use is it?"

"What use is it?" Eggleson repeated. "I don't understand."

"What use is it?" David Mitchell repeated again, his deep voice reaching all corners of the hall, even without a microphone. "What does it do that's important? If it died out, who would miss it? What right does it have to exist?"

Eggleson nodded. "I understand your question now. And I guess I would respond by asking, what right do we have to say it shouldn't exist? Are we that smart? Are you that smart?"

"I'm smart enough to know when somebody's not answering my question."

"Then I'll try to answer it. It has no practical use — at least that we know of now. But we might find one someday. There's an endangered species of tree in South America that turns out to be incredibly useful in the treatment of high blood pressure." Eggleson paused. "This butterfly does have an important use as a tool of scientific study. This species is a missing link in the evolution of butterflies and moths." He looked out at David Mitchell and said, "But I don't think that's liable to impress you much, either."

"To be frank, I don't give a damn about the evolution of butterflies and moths."

"I'll try once more," Dr. Eggleson said. "Just because we're the smartest species on Earth, I don't see why we should assume the power to run the world. I see nature as a complex and beautiful web of life-forms that we have no right to tamper with. Every unique species has unique genes that have taken millions of years to evolve. They're part of a precious gene pool. When a species becomes extinct, the gene pool shrinks. . . . The diversity of nature is cut. . . . We all lose."

"THAT'S SCIENTIFIC GARBAGE!" an older man's voice shouted out near me. Mr. Connally, the white-haired biology teacher and head of the science department at our high school, stood up. "What about the dinosaurs?"

"What about them?" Eggleson asked.

"There weren't any loggers around to cut down their habitat, yet they became extinct." There was a murmur of agreement from the crowd. "I could go on for half an hour naming species that we know once existed from fossil remains, but they're not around today. And you could do it, too. If you teach at Berkeley, you're enough of a scientist to understand that the process whereby species become extinct and new species take their place is perfectly natural. It's not of man. It's of nature or, if you will, of God. It's part of his master plan for this world. Someday the human species will become extinct. You're the one who's trying to control nature by saying we have to step in and meddle to save species whose leases have run out." He sat down, to thunderous applause.

Dr. Eggleson smiled. "I've heard that argument, and it sounds convincing, but it's really not accurate. Sure, species becoming extinct is a part of the natural process. But not the way it's happening in the world today. Not the way it's happening in the Amazon, and in the oceans. Biodiversity is being cut at a rate the world had never seen before. To compare what human beings are doing in a few years to what nature did over millions of years is, as you so nicely put it, scientific garbage. Yes?"

Mary Carson, the head of the Kiowa Women's Club and one of the wealthiest people in our town, had steel-gray hair and a sharp voice. She waited until a microphone was brought to her, and then said, "What I'd like to know is how you found this butterfly? If it only lives in the company forest and you found it there, then you must have been trespassing."

I felt a jolt of fear at her question. Dr. Eggleson retained his calm. "I don't think we'll get anywhere by throwing around accusations that are completely speculative and will probably only have the effect of raising tempers. . . ."

"I'm asking you if you went onto company land and found it yourself?" she demanded, interrupting him.

He was momentarily knocked off balance. His silence came through as a denial.

"If you didn't trespass, then somebody else found it and turned it over to you? Who?"

Complete silence enveloped the big hall. I sank down a few inches in my seat and sat on my hands. I felt something stirring within myself — an impulse, a crazy certainty — that made me shiver with fear and try to hide in my seat. I think most of all I was trying to hide from myself. "It doesn't really matter how I got it," Dr. Eggleson told her, recovering his poise. "The point is that it's here, and we have to decide what to do. Any more questions? Yes?"

Mickey Lane stood up. He was a decent, well-respected man in his late forties. His wife sat next to him, and his six kids, ranging in age from about two to fifteen, seemed to take up a good part of an entire row of seats. "I don't come to Berkeley and try to tell you how to teach and live your life. Where do you get off coming here, to an honest, hard-working town, and telling us what we have to do?"

There was loud applause. People shouted: "Yeah. Tell 'em, Mick."

"I'm not telling you what to do."

"Forgive my language, but you sure as hell are. And we don't need you here. We don't want you here. We're just getting by as it is, and you're asking for a lotta trouble coming here."

The clapping and the shouting were much louder. The crowd was definitely getting stirred up. The policemen edged in a bit from the wings.

"I'm glad you said that," Dr. Eggleson replied when the shouting quieted. "Because it gives me a chance to say something back to you. I'm not afraid of you, or your town, or anything you can try to do to hurt me. I'm here as an American citizen, speaking out and fighting for something that I believe in, and I never ran away from a fight in my life. And *you* excuse *my* strong language, but I'm sure as hell not gonna run from this one."

There were angry shouts in reply, and two young men started for the stage. Dr. Eggleson held his ground, and when they reached the police, the two guys were restrained and escorted out of the hall. Mayor Stokes walked to the microphone. "I guess this has gone about far enough," he said. "We've listened, and we've had a chance to speak, and I don't want things to get out of hand. So I'll say a few words, and Stanley may want to say something, and then I think we'll call it a night."

117

"Professor . . ." He turned to face Eggleson. "Let me be blunt. There are a lot of bugs in the world. They have different-colored wings and different-sized feet, and they make different sounds when you step on them." There was a burst of loud applause mixed with laughter at that, but the mayor held up his hand for silence. "I understand that you earn your money studying those bugs, so you care about them more than most people. Well, I earn my money looking after this town. And let me tell you, a lumber town these days needs some protection, too.

"The men and women out there," and he pointed toward us dramatically, "are an endangered species, just as much as that butterfly. They're honest people. Hard-working people. Decent, church-going, family people. And their way of life is under attack. If you hadn't found this bug, no one would've known about it. Why don't you just put it back where you found it and go bother people someplace else?"

That got a standing ovation. Dr. Eggleson took the microphone back, but he had to wait thirty seconds or so for the applause to die down enough so that he could make himself heard. "I see how you got elected," he said. But no one was laughing at Dr. Eggleson's jokes anymore, and he sensed the change in mood, so he said, "I came here to make a proposal, and I won't back away from it. Work with me or work against me, but things will never be the way they were."

"Well, how do we know this bug of yours doesn't live anyplace else?" the mayor asked. "If it lives here, maybe it lives thirty miles down the road. Or a hundred miles. Maybe there are millions of those things in some forest somewhere that just haven't been discovered. How about that?"

"It's possible," Dr. Eggleson admitted. "But unlikely."

"Yeah? Well it was people like you who found a little fish called the Snail Darter in the Tennessee River and halted work on the Tellico Dam for years. Can't tell you how many jobs were lost and families hurt. And what happened? Why don't you tell us."

"Eventually they found Snail Darters in other streams," Dr. Eggleson said.

"That's right, eventually they did. Whadda ya know." Mayor Stokes paused to allow more applause. "We're not going to let you put us out of business," he said, his voice rising. "Bridal Veil. Wildwood. Covelo. Potter Valley." He tolled out the names of lumber towns that had recently failed like someone announcing passengers who had drowned on a shipwreck. "We're not aiming to join them, Professor. Not for some oversized horsefly you've taken a shine to."

The mayor handed Eggleson back the microphone and walked to his seat, amid thunderous applause. Dr. Eggleson waited, and waited, but it was clear that he was losing his cool. When he finally spoke, he sounded angry. "You don't like butterflies, Mr. Mayor? How do you feel about bald eagles? They were down to less than a hundred, but it looks like we managed to save them. How about California Condors? There are only about fifty left now, all in captivity. We're trying to introduce pairs back into the wild now, but it's a painstaking process. Maybe your grandson will be able to see one in flight. Or if you don't like birds, how about the grizzly bear? Or the American crocodile?"

The mayor refused to take up the argument. He sat there with his arms folded, glancing at Eggleson and looking past him to his townspeople.

The mayor's silence seemed to make Dr. Eggleson even angrier. "I have a better one to tell you about," he almost shouted. He faced the crowd. "When I was a boy, growing up in Oregon, we used to watch the wild salmon runs every year, and I can tell you there was nothing like it. Hell, they'd make jumps and run up rapids that just didn't seem possible. I'm sure many of you've heard of the sockeye salmon. One of the most daring, one of the most noble . . ."

His voice broke for a second, and he took a deep breath. "Hell'uva fish," he continued in a deeper voice. "Six or seven pounds. Males are bright red: females olive. They make a more than nine hundred-mile journey from the Pacific Ocean through the Columbia and Snake rivers to reach their spawning grounds in Idaho. When I was a teenager, which wasn't so long ago, thousands upon thousands of them used to churn up the water. Things have changed since then. We haven't only been over-fishing them and polluting their rivers; we've also been building dams. More than seventy of them — deadly obstacles to the salmon runs.

"In 1989, there were only two sockeye nests sighted at the spawning grounds. Year after that, I was part of a team of scientists and naturalists who went to monitor the crisis in wild salmon runs. Only one sockeye salmon — one" — his voice broke, but he kept on talking, somehow, his tone vibrating with emotion — "made the nine hundred-mile journey to

120

its ancestral spawning grounds. Watching that one solitary, noble fish swim up the river, jumping, fighting the falls, maybe the last of its species . . . trying to breed but truly swimming toward extinction, well" — he turned to the mayor — "I know people and jobs are important, but I think there are things that are more important. And if you don't, then you're shortsighted and you're wrong."

There was a very deep and angry silence. And then Stanley McKeon walked to the front of the stage. Since the McKeon family owns the mill that keeps the town alive, Stanley is, in a sense, the living incarnation of Kiowa. He's a nice man — tall and a bit gaunt, slightly awkward, unassuming and gentle in manner, yet smart and purposeful. He's always reminded me of Abe Lincoln. His father had been immensely popular, and Stanley seemed like he had inherited his father's good qualities along with the mill. I remembered my father saying that Stanley had personally guaranteed to him that the mill would look after my dad's health insurance needs, now that he was sick.

"Since the professor here talked about his childhood, let me go back a little bit further," Stanley began in a restrained tone. "My great-grandfather staked out this land. My grandfather built the first mill, with the help of his two sons. My father — who I think many of you remember as fondly as I do — built the mill up and the town along with it. I'm not planning to be the McKeon who lets it all slip away."

Tumultuous applause. The ovation seemed to shake the hall. Stanley half turned till he was facing Dr. Eggleson, looking him right in the eye.

"This whole discussion has been a farce. The professor here doesn't really care about this butterfly any more than we do. The butterfly is a tool. Just the way the spotted owl was a tool. Just the way the gnat catcher and the Delta smelt are tools. What the professor is really after are the trees. You have to understand this, because if you don't, his proposal makes some sense. Why not work together? I don't have anything against the butterfly. I like butterflies.

"But I'll say it again. What he's really after are our trees. We've seen the pattern again and again, all through this region. The trees are on private land, so the way that environmentalists try to protect them is by finding some rare bug or bird or fish and then appealing for state or federal protection. And if we're dumb enough to let him and a bunch of his friends in to do a study in our forest, we'll be giving them the ammunition to shoot us with. Because, believe me, they'll conclude that logging has to be stopped in our forest, and they'll have a long and detailed study to back it up. And you know what we'll be doing? We'll all be looking for jobs.

"No," he said to Eggleson, "I don't know how you got this butterfly in the first place but we don't want you setting foot in our forest again. It's private land. It's my land. And through me, it belongs to everyone out there who depends on it for their livelihood. Keep out of it, for your own safety. You hear me? You want a fight? You've got one. We've got our lawyers already working on this. We're not going to let you put us out of business, Professor. Not for one ugly butterfly that doesn't even have a name."

"Okay," Dr. Eggleson said. "Have it your way. As a matter of fact, I don't like it that you're cutting old growth, and I don't believe in private land when it contains trees that are thousands of years old. But I wasn't after your trees, and I came here in good faith, and I appreciate your listening. As for this butterfly, well, I suppose you're right; it doesn't have a name. New species are usually named after the people who find them, and I didn't find this one. But it does have a right to live. And I'm going to see . . ."

The professor broke off because he saw me stand up. Our eyes met across the distance of thirty-five feet or so. He shook his head very slightly, telling me to sit back down. But I was in a kind of a trance and nothing I saw or heard could have stopped me.

Maybe it was partly the alcohol — I felt slightly giddy and at the same time wildly exhilarated. Maybe it was the angry conversation I had listened to in the parking lot of the Exxon station and the feeling, which had been growing all week, that these were not my real friends and that I didn't belong among them. Maybe it was Dr. Eggleson's story about the one sockeye salmon swimming up-stream — it had brought tears to my eyes. But most of all, what pushed me to my feet and got me going was an inner knowledge — a certainty — that this was something I had to do for myself, for the real John Rodgers. Up till then, in my life, I had been somebody else, growing up in the wrong family, living in the wrong town, trying to fit in at the wrong school.

This was me.

I was in the aisle now, heading for the stage. I guess everyone saw me — thick silence fell over the townspeople in their folding chairs like a winter quilt. Dr. Eggleson, on the stage, kept shaking his head as I walked closer. "No," he said once out loud. "Sit back down." As I passed the front row and headed for the steps to the stage, my eyes met Miss Merrill's eyes. For the first time since I had known her, she looked very frightened. She also shook her head, urging me to go back and sit down. Her lips were pressed tightly together. She looked very beautiful.

I kept going. The policemen must've understood from my manner that I wasn't going up there to disrupt the meeting. They didn't even try to stop me. Step by step I climbed to the stage, and looked out over the large audience. I turned toward the rostrum and for a second looked right into the face of Stanley McKeon. His usually gentle gray eyes hardened with understanding and then flashed with fury. I stepped to the rostrum, picked up the plastic terrarium, and peered inside. The butterfly was standing on a twig, looking back at me curiously through its compound eyes. "Hi," I whispered, very very low. Or maybe I just thought it. One of the butterfly's wings stirred slightly, as if he were waving in response.

Dr. Eggleson put a heavy hand across my shoulder, and I heard his deep voice boom out, "Well, now it has a name. Order Lepidoptera. Family Lycaenidae. Genus *Plebejus*. Species — Rodgers California Blue."

Chapter Thirteen

"I wish you hadn't done that," Dr. Eggleson said as we roared down Route 6 in his jeep.

"You mean come up on stage? I had to."

"It puts me in a very difficult position."

"Well, you put me in a very difficult position. How do you think I felt when I found out you had called a big town meeting about my butterfly . . . and you didn't even tell me?"

"I've been running around like a madman, talking to experts and setting things up. And to tell you the truth, I thought it might be better for you if I just left you out of things."

"When I gave you the butterfly, you said I should just trust you and there wouldn't be any trouble. That didn't turn out to be exactly true. I had to do what I did."

He nodded. "I guess I understand. Maybe I didn't handle things the best way. But what are we going to do with you?"

"You're not responsible for me."

"Well, that's good," he said with a smile. "Because

if I were, I wouldn't have the slightest idea how to advise you. Want a cup of coffee?"

"No. But I'll take a hot chocolate."

We stopped at a truck stop about twenty miles out of Kiowa. I had hot chocolate and a slice of apple pie, and Dr. Eggleson had a big mug of black coffee. He watched me wolf down the pie and shook his head. "You shouldn't be able to eat like that," he told me.

"This is the first time I've had an appetite in a week."

"Do you realize what you just did?"

"I'm not stupid."

"I didn't say you were stupid. But I think you're pumped up. And when you come back down, you're going to have to face certain realities."

"Like?"

"Like where do we go from here?"

"Just drop me home."

"In Kiowa?"

"That's where I live."

He frowned into the dregs of his black coffee. "I know it is," he whispered. "That's the problem." He took out his thick black wallet and rummaged around till he found a business card. It had his official title, and both his home and work phone numbers and addresses. "I'll take you home after this," he said. "But if you need me, you can reach me at one of those two numbers, or at least leave messages for me. I call in all the time. I do feel some responsibility — quite a bit, in fact — and if there's anything I can do . . . if you have any questions, or you need some advice . . ."

I looked at him. After what had happened in the

126

town hall, I felt completely fearless. "I do have one question."

"Yes? What?"

"Do you like Miss Merrill?"

His big body jerked up slightly in his seat, and I think he might have blushed slightly behind his bushy mustache. It was like watching an embarrassed walrus. "I . . . well . . . of course I do. She was one of my best students."

"And she's a very nice woman."

"Extremely nice," he agreed with noticeable discomfort. "But I don't think we should sit here and talk . . ."

"And she's pretty, too," I said, cutting him off.

His eyes narrowed. "Yes, she's pretty, too. What are you getting at?"

"Nothing. I just said that she was nice and pretty."

"I heard what you said." His enormous right hand wrapped and unwrapped around his coffee mug; it was like a python encircling a small animal. "You know, in some ways you remind me very much of me when I was your age."

I looked across the table at his big barrel chest, broad shoulders, and roughly handsome features. "That's hard to believe. In what way?"

"No one could figure out why I was saying what I was saying, or doing what I was doing."

"But you knew yourself? I mean, there usually was a reason?"

"Sure." He grinned slightly. "I was crazy. That was the reason. Maybe we should take you home now."

I nodded, and he flagged down a waitress and paid the check.

He dropped me off right in front of my house and waited with the motor idling till I had let myself in and shut the door behind me. The big house was silent and empty, exactly the way I had left it. Everything was in its proper place — it didn't seem like anything major had really changed while I'd been away. I checked the answering machine in the kitchen, but there were no messages. My parents in San Francisco must have gone to sleep by now.

I double-locked the front and back doors, checked to see that the windows were all bolted, and then went upstairs. Soon, I was lying in bed, looking out through my window at the sliver of yellow moon. It looked sharp and menacing — a scythe slicing through the midnight. In my mind, I replayed the evening's events. I guess I probably should have felt scared and nervous thinking about what I had done, but I felt calmness and a certain deep satisfaction. It was like the pressure that I had been feeling for the past week or so had been let off. Soon I slipped off into a deep and untroubled sleep.

The next morning, I knew almost as soon as I came down the stairs that there was trouble. The telephone answering machine was blinking with lots of messages. Usually the phone's ring wakes me up, but as I said I had really fallen into a deep sleep the previous night. When I saw all the blinking messages, I thought immediately that something might have happened to my father, and pushed the "Play" button. There were six messages in all, a nasty medley of sober and drunk profanity from different callers. I didn't recognize the voices, but two threatened me by name.

I erased the messages, had a bowl of cereal, and got my school stuff together. After all, it was a Tuesday — a school day. We had a track meet that afternoon. I was still a student at Kiowa High School. On one level, I knew that the previous night had been some kind of a break point in my life; on another level, I had a routine of going to school on weekdays that I had been following for years, and I stubbornly stuck to it. If I didn't show up, the other kids would think I was afraid. I remembered Dr. Eggleson saying from the stage that he'd never run away from a fight in his life. It sounded like a good philosophy.

I got my second unpleasant surprise of the day as I left our house and started down the walk toward the sidewalk. Someone had egged my house during the night. And I don't mean just one or two eggs. I mean fifty or a hundred. The whole front was spattered with dried yolks and shells. I turned away and headed for school. The obscene messages and the eggs had toughened my resolve to show this town I wouldn't be scared away.

After about a block and a half, I spotted Mary Menendez on the opposite site of the street. She was a shy girl who played the flute in the band and never talked much to anyone. She was walking with her head down, but I caught her glancing at me so I gave her a wave and a smile. "Morning."

"Good morning," she said and sped up.

We turned onto Oak and suddenly there were a lot of kids heading toward school. At first they didn't seem to notice me. It was like I was invisible. Then two senior guys cruised slowly by in an old Ford and started honking as they passed me. "Hey, you."

Honk. "HEY. RODGERS." HONKKK. *HONKKK.* "I'm talking to you. Want us to stop this car and get out to talk to you?"

"What do you want?"

"You and your friend were great last night."

I kept walking.

"You're a real big man, now, huh? I'M TALKING TO YOU."

I stopped. "What do you want me to say?"

"Your brothers know what you did? Your father know?"

I started walking again. Suddenly, it seemed as if everyone on the block was watching me.

The blue Ford cruised close to the curb. The senior in the passenger side opened the door and got out. His first name was Troy, and he was the starting center on the football team. "Where do you think you're going?"

"To school." I put my head down and kept walking.

"Yeah?" he said. "Yeah? I don't think so."

I heard him coming and couldn't stop myself from turning toward the footsteps.

One punch. I didn't even feel it hit me. Just the smash of impact, and then the lights blinked off. When they came on again, I was on the ground holding my nose, and Mary Menendez was kneeling next to me, holding a Kleenex. I took the tissue and touched my face with it. It came away red with blood. "Is my nose broken?" I asked her.

She hesitated and then peeked. She shook her head. "I don't think so. But it's bleeding bad."

I tried to get up.

"I don't think you should go to school."

My books were lying all over a lawn — I guess after Troy hit me, he kicked my schoolbooks around. I got everything back together as best I could and set off for school again, clutching the tissue to my nose.

About a block from school I ran into Rhino and Gus Daly and three of my other track teammates. They were the same guys I had drunk beers and hung out with behind the Exxon station the previous night. When they saw me, they bunched together into a tight little silent pack and walked on together, as if I had a contagious disease. Rhino glanced back at me once, and our eyes met. He shook his head very slightly. Then he ignored me like the rest of them. I had known him since kindergarten and had always respected his judgment and appreciated his good nature. Seeing him shake his head and then ignore me hurt a lot more than getting a bloody nose.

I neared the school. There were ten minutes till the first homeroom bell, and everyone was walking quickly. I stayed about fifteen feet behind my teammates. If they didn't want to talk to me, I wasn't going to force the issue, but I was going the same place they were and nobody was going to stop me. I guess word had spread that I was coming because as I neared the edge of the schoolgrounds, I saw four or five of the toughest guys in my class standing with their hands on their hips. I knew them all, and I knew that they were waiting for me.

I felt myself slow. My mouth was dry, and I swallowed several times. For some reason, fear tastes hard and metallic, like copper pennies. *Okay*, I thought, *okay. Calm, be calm. Whatever happens, do not hit back.* They had taken their hands off their hips and stood with their arms dangling down toward the dirt. The grass of the school lawn started about twenty feet behind them. *You will not hit back. It won't do any good. You have a right to go to school. Keep walking. Calm. Calm. Almost there.*

I was pushed, but I stayed up. Somebody shoved me again, and laughed. A girl's voice started saying "Stop, don't . . ." and a guy shouted, "No, keep going. Kick his butt." I kept walking. I was about ten feet from the grass now. It gleamed in the morning sunshine, a thick emerald welcome mat. A leg tripped me from behind, and I went down to my knees on the hard-packed dirt. *Back up. Almost there. Back up.* A foot caught me in the small of my back and knocked me sprawling.

So I crawled for that green welcome mat on my hands and knees. A kick crashed into my rib cage, but somehow I was still moving forward. A boot stomped down on my fingers. A toe swung at my jaw — a glancing blow. The green grass receded. Sounds merged together. Was it Miss Merrill's voice from far away shouting, "Stop that now! STTTTOOOOPPP"? Could it really be only four or five guys doing this to me? Or was it the whole school joining in the fun? Or the whole town? I reached the haven of green grass and was slammed face first into it. Then a real kick — the kind that cracks ribs. My mouth jerked open, and I tasted the grass. Another kick.

"Let him alone." It was Rhino's voice, but I never saw him. All I know is that suddenly I was back up on my feet, my schoolbooks gone, my fists pumping, not in fight but in flight. I was running away from school. Tears were streaming down my face, and I never slowed or looked back to see if anyone was following me.

It had taken such a beating to change a distance runner into a sprinter.

Chapter
Fourteen

There are times when you think, and then there are times when you only react.

I ran to the bank and used my card to take three hundred dollars, the daily machine withdrawal limit, out of my savings account. A few minutes later, I found myself on the back seat of a bus, headed out of town. No luggage. No change of clothes. The bus was nearly empty, and the back seat smelled of orange peel. Then I was in the bus depot of a larger town, watching an eight-year-old play a video game. Then on another bus. Heading south. And west.

It was good not to think. I watched the scenery change out the window. Towns separated by forests gave way to small cities separated by suburbs. We popped out on the coast near Fort Bragg, and the Pacific Ocean was a light violet-blue in the noon sunshine. The Golden Gate, incredibly long and impossibly beautiful, spanned the water from Marin to San Francisco. Even though it was a workday, San Francisco Bay was dotted by sailboats, running and tacking before the gentle breeze. From the height of the bridge it was just possible to see the white wakes their hulls traced in the sheet of blue.

I got off at the Main Terminal and began to walk. I don't know the city all that well, but it didn't matter because I wasn't going anywhere special. In fact, I was sort of eager to get lost, which is a nice way to walk if you have the time. I plodded the length of Chinatown, stopping to inspect the strange-looking fruits and vegetables on display in the markets: mangoes, gingerroot, Chinese cabbages, and lots of ones I didn't know. I climbed higher and higher. I passed four-star hotels with doormen in livery, waiting on the steps, and a lovely church whose bells chimed the three o'clock hour.

Could they all have been wrong? Could a whole school or a whole town be wrong? Could my parents and all my friends be wrong? No. I must be the one who was wrong. Or were questions of right and wrong a stupid way to look at it? Did anything matter, now, anyway? What more could I do to them or them to me? Better not to think about it. Just keep climbing . . . to the top of the city. I found myself on Telegraph Hill, looking down from Coit Tower at a panoramic view of the bay. I was out of breath, and even though it was cold, my arms and legs were damp with sweat.

I headed back down by another route. *Yes, it's better just to coast downhill and not think. Better to let gravity do all the work.* I reached Fisherman's Wharf. The souvenir shops and seafood restaurants were mostly empty on this weekday afternoon. I bought myself a bag of fried shrimp and chips and walked along the edge of the wharf, enjoying the salt tang in the air and the rippling reflections of city sky-scrapers in oily-smooth water.

I killed a few hours doing every stupid tourist thing I could think of. I took a tour of an authentic World War II submarine docked at the wharf. It's amazing to see how small the living quarters were, and to imagine a group of men sharing the tiny bunk-rooms and work stations and dining room for month after month, living beneath the ocean in constant danger. In a way, there must be something nice and simple about growing up during wartime — espe-cially a world war like the last one. You get drafted. You have to fight. It's the right thing to do. All your decisions are made for you.

I walked through the Ripley's Believe It or Not Museum, and the Wharf Aquarium, spending a few hours with bearded ladies and two-headed dogs, friendly dolphins, and hungry-looking sharks. *Any-thing not to think*. The sun was already setting when I headed away from the waterfront. I followed side streets randomly, walking briskly and enjoying the way the afternoon light muted the bright blues and reds and whites of the buildings.

It was almost dark when I saw a quaint, two-story, Victorian-style white building with a hand-painted sign that read: LOST TRAVELER HOTEL. The name sounded very appropriate, given the fact that I didn't have the slightest idea where I was or what I was even doing in San Francisco. My legs were tired, and I was getting cold, so I headed up the walk. A smaller sign, hanging above the doorway, pro-claimed: CLEAN, REASONABLE RATES, COLOR TV IN EVERY ROOM.

Bells tinkled as I came through the door. The little hotel looked homey and cheerful. There were lovely hardwood floors with brightly colored throw rugs, and original paintings of city views and seascapes on the walls. I stopped at what appeared to be the front desk and waited for someone to come. At the end of the hallway I could see a parlor with antique furniture and wooden rockers, and a wood fire blazing orange-red. "Hello?" I called. "Excuse me. Hello?"

A short, white-haired woman hurried out of a side room, wiping her hands on her light blue bib. I guess she had been cooking something. "Yes?" she said.

"Do you have any rooms?"

"I'll take it, Martha," a male voice said. She headed back into the kitchen and a moment later, a very tall old man with bushy white eyebrows and a completely bald head emerged from another doorway, ducking his head slightly so as not to hit the lintel. He walked to the desk, flipped open a leatherbound guest book, and gave me a smile. "Welcome."

"Hi."

As he examined me, his smile slowly changed to a look of concern, and then even a slight frown of distrust. "What happened to you?"

I guess my face was pretty badly marked up from the beating I had taken back in Kiowa that morning. I had washed the blood off in a bus terminal bathroom, but my nose had swelled up, and one of my eyes was dark and puffy. "I need a room," I told him.

"Are you . . . okay?"

"Do you have room for me or not?"

He bent closer to my face, studying my bruises.

"What are you, seventeen? Eighteen?" His voice was soft and high-pitched. "Doesn't look like the nose is broken. Who did that to you?"

"Okay, forget it," I said. "Sorry to bother you." I turned and made it halfway to the door before I felt his hand on my shoulder.

I let him turn me around. Up close, he seemed even taller. No wonder he had chosen an old hotel with high ceilings. "I have a room," he said. "Single. Color TV. Forty dollars." He saw me hesitate. "I was just doing my job, asking you those questions. If you were messed up with drugs, or . . . well, we don't need certain kinds of business. That's all."

I hesitated and then followed him back to the desk and filled out a room registration form. While I wrote, I could feel his eyes continue to study me. "Here's the forty."

"You can pay when you check out."

"Take it now."

He gave me back a receipt and a key. "It's on the second floor. I'll show you up. Don't you have any luggage?" I shook my head, and he raised his bushy white eyebrows. "Just the clothes you're wearing?"

"That's right."

"Okay," he said with a slight smile. "That will make it easier going up the stairs. C'mon."

The stairs were narrow and steep. It looked like there were about half a dozen second-floor bedrooms, all opening off the same long corridor. Mine was at the very end. "You're gonna get a nice view," the old man said, fumbling to open the door. "No extra charge. Here, take a look."

He opened the door, and we stepped in. It was small and neat — a bed, a writing desk, an oak chest

138

of drawers, and a tiny bathroom. He walked over to the window and pulled the curtains apart to show me the view of the bay. "See?"

"Great. Thank you."

"One of the nicest rooms we have."

"Yup."

He walked to the door and stood with his hand on the knob, looking back into the room at me. "If you want, I can get you some Band-Aids and some disinfectant to wash those cuts with."

"No, I'm fine. I'm gonna go out and get some dinner. Bye."

"We have a little hotel restaurant of our own. Martha cooks some of the best food you'll ever taste."

"I feel like taking a walk. I'll find someplace to eat on the way. Thanks. Bye."

He shook his head and closed the door. I walked to the window. The neon of waterfront hotels and restaurants spilled out over the dark water in a flickering rainbow. I wondered if my mother's hotel was nearby, and if she were looking out at the same view. I could call her. Or go see her. *And tell her what? If I went, I would only increase her pain and worry. Surely she was suffering enough without hearing from me and about me.* Instead, I washed up in the sink and headed out for a walk and some dinner.

I came down the stairs quietly, hoping to sneak out, but the tall hotel manager caught me by the front door. "I don't mean to bug you," he said, "but it gets cold here at night. Let me lend you a jacket."

"Don't bother."

"C'mon," he said. "I'm sorry I asked you so many questions. At least take my jacket. It won't fit you, but it'll keep you warm."

"Okay."

It was red flannel and much too long — it nearly came down to my knees. "You can roll up the sleeves," he said helpfully. "Don't worry about the length. People in this city wear all kinds of weird things."

"Thanks," I told him. "See you later." And I was out the door before he could talk to me anymore. It had grown much colder. I rolled the sleeves up as I walked — the bottom of the jacket reached down to my knees like a trench coat. San Francisco looked beautiful by night; car headlights moving up and down the steep hills glittered like swarming lightning bugs.

I decided to eat in Chinatown, and walked by two or three touristy-looking restaurants with carved dragons out in front and lots of American customers visible through the window. Finally, on a narrow street that wasn't much more than an alley, I saw a small place with Formica tables and a menu in the window that hadn't been translated into English. I walked in. The smell was terrific — ginger and fried noodles and soy. All the other customers were Chinese, and they really seemed to be enjoying themselves. There were many large families, each at its own round table, with adults and even small children all laughing and talking and spooning helpings of food from enormous platters.

I sat by myself at a small table near the door. A young waiter came over to me, carrying a pot of tea and a cup. He looked about my age. "Do you know what you want?"

I was glad he could speak English. "Some hot-and-sour soup and a plate of . . . whatever you think I'd like."

140

He looked at me. "Spicy?"

"Not too hot, please."

"Beef, chicken, pork, seafood?"

"Chicken."

"You like noodles?"

"Sure."

He headed back into the kitchen and I sat alone with my forearms up on the smooth Formica, enjoying being on my own. Maybe that was the answer. Maybe I should just cut myself loose for a while and travel around the country. I was smart enough and hard-working enough to find jobs. It was a romantic daydream. I wouldn't have any worries or responsibilities — I could just go wherever the road took me.

The hot-and-sour soup was delicious, and the large dish of chicken, vegetables, and fried noodles that the waiter brought next was also excellent. As I ate, I contemplated the alternative to running away. I would have to go to my parents here in San Francisco. First to my mother, at her hotel. Somehow, without alarming her too much, I would have to explain what had happened back in Kiowa. Then, together, we would have to find a way to tell my father. They would want me to go back and take my final exams, and finish out the school year. The thought of returning to Kiowa made me angry — if I ever went back, I wanted it to be on my terms.

I paid for the meal and left a nice tip. The walk home was quite cold, and I was thankful for the heavy jacket. My legs were tired from walking so much and climbing so many hills, and my ribs ached where I had been kicked and stomped on that morning.

The tall hotel manager must have been watching for me, because he met me by the door. "Find a good dinner?"

"Yeah. Thanks for your jacket."

"The other guests have gone to bed. Martha's also turned in early. So it's just the two of us awake. I'll be going up myself in twenty minutes or so. Do you want a cup of tea before bed?"

"No, thanks."

"Just a quick cup," he said. "The fire's still going, and the tea's already made. I need somebody to talk to while I drink it."

I tried to refuse several more times, but I ended up following him into the comfortable living room. We sat on rockers, facing the fire. The smell of wood-smoke from the fireplace reminded me of home. The tall old man poured me a cup of tea. "What'd you eat?"

"Chinese. Noodles."

"I like Chinese myself," he said. "I have a dim sum place I go to every Sunday morning. You like dim sum?"

"Sure," I said. I had no idea what dim sum were.

"This is my favorite room in the hotel. Martha and I did all the decorating ourselves. Sometimes you never quite figure out how a room should look, but this one came out just right."

"Is Martha your wife?"

"Girlfriend."

It seemed strange to hear such an old man talk about a woman as his girlfriend. But, after all, this was San Francisco, the city of alternative life-styles. As long as they were happy together, it was none of my business whether they chose to get married or not. For a while we sipped tea in silence and watched the dying fire.

"Want to talk about it?" he finally asked.

"What?"

"You know what."

"You mean what I'm doing here? No, I don't want to talk about it."

"Okay. Fair enough. Could I tell you something about myself, though?"

"You can say anything you want."

"There's one movie that always gets me," he said. "Always has. *The Wizard of Oz*. You wouldn't think a man as old as I am would cry when he sees a kids' movie, but that one always brings tears."

A long silence. Our rockers made slight creaking noises as they moved back and forth on the old wooden floor. He kept glancing at me. Finally, I felt like I had to say something. "Am I supposed to ask why that movie makes you cry? Something about there being no place like home? Because if that's where you're heading, I'd rather not get into it."

He smiled. "Okay, either you're real smart or I'm transparent. You cut me right off at the pass. That is where I was heading. You show up here with no luggage, face a mess, clearly upset — I've seen it before. I used to work at a Holiday Inn near the bus station, and every once in a while I'd see it."

"What?"

"Nice kid from a small town arriving in the city. Sixteen. Seventeen. Usually a girl. Sometimes they'd been beat up; sometimes the scars didn't show. Little or no luggage. A small bankroll they'd brought from home. Couple of hundred dollars or so. They'd get off the bus and take a room at the

143

Inn and figure they'd find a job or something soon."

He paused and scratched his head. "Now the smartest ones, or maybe I should say the luckiest ones, would sleep on it a night or two, and then turn around and go back home. Because whatever happened to them back in that small town wasn't nothing compared to what can happen to a nice innocent kid in a big city. But the dumbest ones . . ."

I started to stand up. "I'm going to bed."

He surprised me by grabbing the arm of my rocker and raising it up so that I slipped back into the seat. "Look, I don't know you," he said. "I got no reason to do this except I'm trying to help. Just listen for one more minute."

"One more," I agreed. "You were talking about the dumb ones."

"Like me," he said. "Ran away from my own small town to join the army. Got stationed in Yokosuka, Japan. After that, I knocked around Asia for years. Japan. Thailand. Philippines. You bet I had a reason not to write or call or visit the States and see how my old man and old lady were doing. By the time I did, it was too late. Old man was gone. Old lady had mostly lost her mind and didn't know me from Adam. Anyway, what I'm trying to tell you . . ."

He let go of the arm of my rocker and finished his speech in a quick whisper. "If it was something you did, they'll forgive you. That's what it is to be family. No matter what, they'll forgive. And if it was something they did to you, dig into your own heart and find the room to forgive. 'Cause there's no place like home. No place like family. No place like childhood friends."

I stood up. "My friends are the ones who beat me up. Thanks for the tea."

I headed up to my room and in a few minutes, I was all washed up and in bed, beneath a thick coverlet. It was surprisingly quiet for a big city. I left the curtains to the window open, and lying in bed I could see a few lights from tall buildings. The room smelled faintly of lemon air freshener. I thought about what the old hotel owner had been trying to get across.

I like *The Wizard of Oz* as much as the next guy, but if there were really no place like home, then I was in a lot of trouble. Dorothy hadn't had her house egged. If she'd been beaten up by her classmates right on the grounds of her school in Kansas, she might have chosen to stay in Oz.

On the other hand, the old man was probably right about family. I didn't need him to tell me that if you turn your back on your own kin, you never quite recover. I felt the truth of it in my bones. If my family chose not to understand or forgive, then at least the burden of guilt would be on them and not on me. I had to try. Tomorrow I would call my mother at her hotel and explain what had happened. Maybe she would know how to handle it and what to do next. If my father was very ill, it might be better not to tell him anything for a while.

Mom would know.

Time, they say, heals all things. I didn't know if it was true or not, but it was a comforting thought.

My ribs ached when I tried to sleep on my side, so I rolled over onto my stomach and listened to the silence of the old hotel. A few more days like the last two and I would be ready for the nuthouse. The strange thing was that even though I felt terrible about everything that had happened, I didn't regret any decisions I had made. Except, maybe, just one. When they had kicked me and punched me and stepped on me outside Kiowa High School, I regretted lying on the ground and taking it.

It made me angry to think of it. Furious.

I wished I had thrown at least one punch back.

Not that I could have hurt anyone, or gotten them to stop or changed the outcome of the experience one iota. It would have ended exactly the same way. Pacifism is a beautiful thing in principle. I'm sure violence never did a bit of good in the world, and that an eye for an eye and a tooth for a tooth is a primitive and barbaric code of justice.

But when a bunch of guys set out to stomp on you, there's a lot to be said for throwing a punch or two back.

Chapter Fifteen

The next morning, bright and early, I tried to call my mother at her hotel. Three times I tried, and three times I put the receiver back into its cradle when I heard a ring at the other end. It was just too much to explain over the phone. So I decided to go find her hotel and tell her in person.

Mom's hotel, the Bay View, was listed in the yellow pages. There was a map of San Francisco in a drawer of my room's desk — Mom's hotel turned out to be fairly close to where I was staying. I headed downstairs, said good-bye to the tall old man, who tried to get me to stay for a free breakfast, and set off through the bustling streets. It wasn't even eight o'clock yet, but people were already heading off to work, climbing onto buses, clinging to cable cars, and steering cars through the tightly bunched traffic. I guess cities wake up a little earlier than I had thought.

I didn't stop for breakfast; I was too nervous to be hungry. I had no idea what words I would use to tell my mom and how she would react. As I neared her hotel, my fear began to recede until I was just eager to get it over with. She was my mother and she would understand. I almost ran the final two blocks.

The Bay View Hotel was big and new and ugly, but I guess Mom hadn't been thinking about aesthetics when she chose the place. Looking at the glass and imitation marble facade, I hated to think of her coming back to this cold and foreboding box after spending long days with my father in his hospital room. If my father hadn't been responding to treatment, or if his condition had worsened, I could see how this place would just add to her depression.

Maybe she would actually be glad to see me.

I entered and hurried to the clerk at the front desk. He was young and tall, with a uniform that didn't seem to fit and a bad case of acne. "Could you tell me what room Meg Rodgers is in?"

"You missed her."

"She's already left for the day?"

"Checked out."

"When?"

" 'Bout an hour or so ago. Maybe a little more. Just when I came on duty."

"Do you know why?"

He looked at me — I guess it was a strange question.

"I mean, do you have any idea where she was going?"

The clerk shrugged. "She didn't tell me."

Suddenly I was really worried about my father. Had something terrible happened? "Can I use your phone to make a local call? It's kind of an emergency."

I guess he saw from my face that I was telling the truth. "Just make it quick."

I called the hospital and asked for my father's room. "I'm sorry," the receptionist said. "There's no one by that name . . ."

I cut her off. "I'm his son. What happened to him?"

I could hear the rustling of papers on the other end of the line. "He was discharged this morning."

"Discharged? From the hospital?"

"Yes," she said. "He's gone home."

"Then he's . . . okay?"

"If we discharged him, he probably doesn't need hospital treatment anymore. I have to take another call."

"Bye," I said, and hung up.

I stood there in the lobby of the hotel, thoroughly confused. The young clerk gave me a look. "Are you okay?"

"Sure," I said. "Thanks." I walked back out into the sunshine and sat down on a corner bench. A bus stopped, and the driver gestured for me to get on. I waved him away, and he drove off shaking his head angrily. I sat there alone, watching the traffic pass. I guess it was rush hour. The intersection was jammed. Now and then, people sat down on the bench next to me. Buses stopped, and the bench emptied. I sat there and tried to think.

The hospital had discharged my father. He must be okay, at least for the time being. Right about now my parents would be pulling into the driveway and seeing their house with a hundred or so eggs splattered on it. Dad would probably call the police, while Mom would run to talk to the neighbors. Within five minutes they would know the whole story.

I wished they could have heard it from my lips, instead of finding it out from neighbors and towns-people who thought I was a louse and a traitor. Sitting on the bench, I could imagine my father's face when he heard what had happened in the town hall. The muscles beneath his cheeks would harden, and his black eyes would flash with anger. The mill had been his life, and I had struck a powerful blow against it.

I could have found the courage to tell them the story here in San Francisco, away from it all. But it was different now that they had found the truth out for themselves in their own egged house. They were back in the town I had run away from; we were looking at the same event from two different vantage points in two totally different worlds. I sat on the bench and watched the traffic without a clue what to do next.

Cars whizzed past, honking and swerving, as com-muters hurried to get to work. This was just a normal weekday — a Wednesday like any other Wednesday. It was strange to think that no matter what troubles I faced in my own life, the world went on with its normal routine. Back in Kiowa, the high school day was starting. My desk would be empty in home-room. No doubt in fifth-period biology, Miss Merrill would wonder where I was. Perhaps she would call my parents, and they would admit that they didn't know, either.

She would think I was a psycho. I remembered what Dr. Eggleson had said about himself at my age: that he had done things no one could understand and that seemed totally crazy. Yet he had grown up to be a Berkeley professor. Maybe there was hope for me in the far future.

I realized that I did know someone in this city after all. Dr. Eggleson taught across the bay — he had given me his card and told me to call him if I ever needed help. The big entomologist had actually caused a lot of my trouble — why shouldn't I take him up on his offer? It wasn't as if I had a lot of better things to do.

I took a bus over the Bay Bridge. In a few minutes we were in the city of Berkeley, cruising down tree-lined streets. It seemed like one whole part of the city was just an enormous campus — there were lots of students with backpacks and professorial types on bicycles and we must have passed half a dozen bookstores and coffee shops. The people generally looked smart and interesting, if a little weird.

It looked like a place where I could be happy.

I got off at the main campus and found my way to Professor Eggleson's office building. Just as I was approaching the secretary to ask about him, Dr. Eggleson himself came out from a row of offices, zipping up a blue windbreaker around his barrel chest. When he saw me, he stopped walking for a moment, very surprised. Then he smiled. "Hey. John. What are you doing here?"

"Just passing through."

He looked at my face. Some of the bruises had healed a bit overnight, but others had gotten worse. "What happened to you?"

I shrugged. "Not too many insect lovers left in Kiowa."

Guilt showed clearly in his eyes. "Come with me."

We started walking. He glanced at my cuts and bruises several times. "Would you like me to take you to a doctor?"

"Not necessary. It just looks bad, but it's nothing serious."

"Who did that to you?"

"My school chums."

We left the building and walked into the open air in silence. "That's why I didn't tell you when I called the town meeting," he said. "That's why I tried my best to keep you out of it. My God, I'm sorry. I don't know what to say."

"You don't have to say anything. Where are we going?"

"Do you know what's been happening at the lumber mill?" I shook my head. "Well, they're in a bad spot. Legally we're gonna nail them, and they know it. It won't take long to get a court restraining order prohibiting them from cutting timber till the status of the butterfly is ruled on. Once we get that restraining order, the trees and everything that lives in them will be protected for a while, and we can breathe easier."

"That probably doesn't make them very happy at the mill."

"No, they're fighting it every step of the way in court. But, also, they've tripled the cutting of old-growth timber. They want to get their most valuable assets cut before the courts step in and freeze everything."

I thought I had suffered so much in the past few days that I couldn't possibly feel any new pain, but that got me. I loved those three-thousand-year-old trees. I had run through the groves of old growth in countless late afternoon jogs, caught butterflies against their trunks, fished for trout in their shadows. In trying to protect one species of blue butterfly that really might not have been in any danger, I had apparently been the agent of destruction of many old giants of the forest.

Dr. Eggleson looked at me and read my mind. "It had to work out this way," he said. "In the end, it will be a good thing."

"But those giant sequoias . . ."

"We're going to do what we can to save them. I belong to a couple of groups that have been set up for situations just like this. People who are willing to put their lives on the line to protect old forests."

I stopped walking. "Eco-terrorists?"

He smiled. "That's what they call them in your neck of the woods."

"You're gonna go spike trees and stuff?"

"I don't know exactly," he said. "I'm on my way to a meeting right now."

"You mean we are."

He shook his head. "Absolutely not. I've done too much damage to you as it is."

"You haven't done anything to me. I've done it to myself."

"Okay," he said. "Here it is straight. After this meeting, we're driving to Kiowa. This afternoon. There'll be a confrontation with the mill people. We're gonna march outside, maybe force an entry, maybe have a sit-in. There's a good chance there'll be violence. There's no way I can let you come."

My anger about what had happened to me on the school grounds in Kiowa had been growing stronger and stronger. I hated the fact that I had run away.

153

The idea of going back there with people who believed what I believed, and taking a stand with them was enormously compelling. "There's no way you can stop me."

"But . . . it doesn't make sense."

"It's the only thing that makes sense."

"It's gonna be a confrontation. It may get violent."

"I heard you up on the stage say you've never run away from a fight in your life. Why do you want me to run away from one?"

He chewed his mustache. "What I said up there was . . . just a speech. You can't believe what people say when they make speeches. John, that's your hometown."

"It stopped being my town yesterday morning at about eight o'clock." I touched my bruised face. "I still love my parents, but, as for the town . . . yesterday I just lay down and took all the punches. I regret that. I want a chance to take the offensive. I want a chance to go back there and show them that I'm not afraid."

"No," he said, and then louder, "NO. You don't understand what's going on here. You're too close to it. You've lost perspective."

"I KNOW EXACTLY WHAT'S GOING ON HERE," I told him, my voice rising to match his. "This is turning into a war. You've got a side. The people at the mill, and the guys who beat me up . . . they all have sides." My loud voice rang with urgency and desperate conviction. "You can't stop me from choosing a side, too. You can't leave me out in no-man's-land."

Chapter Sixteen

I had expected mostly men, so I was surprised by the number of women. There were even some small kids running around, goofing off and playing hide-and-go-seek. The laughing kids were a real strange ingredient to the mix, because there was something about the meeting that struck me as far more dangerous than anything I had done before.

We met in a big old house in the Oakland Hills. I don't know whose house it was, and I quickly understood that at meetings like this, nobody asks such questions. There were about twenty-five people already there when we arrived, and a dozen or so more arrived after us in twos and threes. A tall man at the door welcomed Professor Eggleson and gave me a curious look.

"He's okay," Eggleson said.

"Yeah?" There was a lot asked in the one-word question.

"Yeah."

None of the people in the big house were acting

particularly nervous, but an undercurrent of shared risk ran from room to room like electricity. I'd say the ages ranged from seven to eighty-five — there was one old man with a gentle smile and a long white beard who looked like he should be selling a health food cereal on TV. Most of the people were college students and graduate students; they were wearing jeans and cotton shirts and they all seemed to know each other pretty well. Needless to say, I didn't see any leather jackets or fur coats — this was a hard-core environmental crowd.

We all gathered in the main living room. Without a word being spoken, the chattering gradually died down. A young man — he couldn't have been more than twenty-seven or twenty-eight — took control of the meeting. I was impressed by how calm he was, and by how smart he looked. I've never seen anyone who just *looked* brilliant before. His brown eyes glowed, as if there were tiny lights behind the irises. He had long brown hair that was tied behind him in a neat ponytail. "Listen up, everybody," he said. "Probably there's no need to say this, but I'll say it anyway. Everything you do from here on could get you in a lot of trouble, so be careful and be thoughtful. If you decide not to come, no one here will blame you. The decisions are yours, and you have to accept the responsibility for them."

There was silence in the big room. You could hear the laughter of the kids playing tag out in the back-yard, and the ticking of a grandfather clock in the hallway.

"Okay," the young leader continued, "let's talk about security. You all know the FBI is interested in who we are and what we do. There may be an undercover agent right here in this room." We all looked around at each other, and there were lots of nervous smiles. "I know it sounds farfetched, but it's quite possible. So don't use last names or write down addresses, and remember that this meeting never took place and none of you know about this house. After we break up, don't talk to your friends or even your family about where we're going or what we're doing this afternoon. Okay?"

There came a chorus of yesses.

The girl on my right tried to pass me a plate of blue corn chips, but I was so fascinated by the clandestine meeting that she had to tap me on the arm three times before I turned to look at her. "Want some?" she whispered.

"No thanks." I took the plate from her and passed it along to the guy on my left, who was playing chess on a miniature set with the guy next to him. It was amazing to me that people could eat snacks and play games at such a meeting. My heart was thumping against my ribs.

"The purpose of this protest will be to attract attention to the accelerated cutting of old-growth trees at the Kiowa mill. Since our protest will interfere with a shift, we may manage to save a few trees today."

"Amen, brother," someone called out.

"We're not looking for violence or trouble with the law, but you have to expect it and be ready for it. I'll say it again: Everybody who heads there with us is making a personal choice to be in danger." He paused just a second for the warning to sink in. "We'll drive to the town of Kiowa separately in five or six cars, park separately, and link up a mile or so from the mill at the intersection of Sylvan and Beech."

"Excuse me," I called out. Everyone looked at me. I found that I had raised my hand, like a student trying to get the attention of his teacher. Feeling foolish, I lowered it. "It's not called Beech anymore. It's called James McKeon Boulevard now."

He studied me. "Are you sure?"

"Mr. McKeon used to own the mill. When he died last year, they renamed the street for him."

The young leader looked at Dr. Eggleson, who nodded. "Okay," the leader said. "Thank you. Make that the corner of Sylvan and James McKeon Boulevard. At three-thirty. Bring whatever signs and banners you want. I have a few special ones already made up. At three-forty on the dot, we start marching to the mill. The story will be called in to TV stations and newspapers just in time for them to get people out to cover our protest. There should be a few reporters and camera crews waiting for us at the front gate. The more publicity the better. Also, media presence will give us some protection.

"We'll march back and forth for a while, chanting and waving signs and generally having fun. And then we'll link arms and sit down in front of the mill entrance. The afternoon shift at the mill will finish at four-thirty" — he looked at me and grinned slightly — "Right?"

"Right."

"They're on triple shift, and the idea is to block the third shift coming in and the second shift coming out. If there's a confrontation, that's when it will happen. The news crews will definitely be there by then, and we should generate some good publicity whatever happens. Remember, they can't cut trees after dark, so the more we hold up the third shift, the fewer sequoias get cut today.

"At that point, the planned part of the protest is over. You can go home. You can sit there longer. You can climb over the fence and hug a tree. You can bring a spike along and leave a little souvenir that a chain saw won't dare go near. But, remember, if you do spike a tree, mark it. Otherwise, a logger might get killed by mistake and we don't want that."

"Speak for yourself," a serious-faced girl shouted.

"Let's not argue. What I'm trying to say is that after the sit-in part of the protest, everybody has to make their own decision what they want to do next. There's likely to be violence, and we can't count on the local police. We have a good lawyer standing by. If you're arrested, he should have you out within twenty-four hours. So be cool. Questions?"

There were none.

"Suggestions?"

None.

"Okay, I've got maps for all the drivers up here. See you in Kiowa."

The big room emptied out fast. Dr. Eggleson was one of the drivers, so he got a map and talked to a few people who were planning to go in his jeep. When they had the details squared away, we headed out. We had just left the house when a voice called, "Hey, wait a sec." It was the young leader. He hurried out of the big house and caught up with us on the long gravel driveway. "We didn't get a chance to meet," he said to me. "I'm Mark." He held out his hand.

"John."

159

Up close, his brown eyes were even brighter. His gaze flicked to my face and quickly examined my cuts and bruises. "I'm gonna break my own rules and ask you a question about yourself. You don't have to answer. You seem to know a lot about the town of Kiowa. . . ."

"I grew up there."

"I figured. What I can't understand is what you're doing here?" He gave Dr. Eggleson a questioning glance.

"John is the one who found the butterfly," Dr. Eggleson told him in a low whisper. "He turned it over to me."

Mark understood instantly, and his gaze was suddenly full of respect. "Holy cow," he said, and gave a low whistle. "No wonder they beat you up. And now you want to go back there with us? Why?"

"Round one wasn't so good. I'm ready for round two."

He grinned slightly. "Why don't you come with me? The professor's got a pretty full jeep, but I'm driving up all by myself. I'm gonna get there a little early and scout the place out. Be helpful to have you along."

"Okay," I said. I turned to Dr. Eggleson. "See you up there."

"Yeah," he said without enthusiasm. And then to Mark, "Will you do me a favor?"

"What?"

"Talk him out of coming."

Mark looked into my eyes and then smiled and shook his head at Dr. Eggleson. "Forget it, Hammond. He's ready for round two."

Twenty minutes later I was in the passenger seat

of Mark's little two-door Toyota Corolla, speeding back toward Kiowa. Mark's car had stickers all over the back bumper that said things like SAVE THE WHALES, FRIEND OF THE OZONE LAYER, GREENPEACE, I BRAKE FOR ANIMALS, and HAWKSBILL TURTLE LOVER. He drove very well and very quickly. At the meeting he had cautioned us to keep silent, but in person he turned out to be surprisingly talkative, and we chatted the whole drive up.

Mark was earning his Ph.D. in astrophysics and wanted to be an astronomer. He had done his undergrad at M.I.T., and spent two years at Oxford on a Fulbright. I felt like a dummy sitting there next to such a brilliant person. I figured anything I'd say would probably sound stupid to him, so I tried to ask a lot of questions and let him do the talking. "How did you get to be the leader of the group?"

"I've been involved with activist environmental groups for a long time," he told me. "First on the East Coast, and then out here. I'm pretty well plugged into sort of a loose national network of strategists and organizers. At the university we have a lot of supporters who don't like the organizational side of things, so gradually I've just taken over that role. Not as if I want to."

"Why don't you?"

"Because when you're an organizer, you become political. And politics is always corrupt. Also, being one of the leaders is dangerous."

"You mean like what you were talking about at the meeting when you warned people about the FBI?"

He nodded. "We operate outside the law. At times we challenge it; at times we have to break it. As much

161

as possible I try to reduce everything to the level of individual responsibility. I never directly tell anyone to break a law. If they want to, that's up to them. But even so — I'm running a big risk. I've been thrown in jail twice and I don't like it. It scares me."

"You don't seem like you would be scared."

"Everyone gets scared. Fear is a basic human emotion. I've tried to learn to control it. But every time I'm in a confrontation, I have to struggle with myself not to turn and run away. I think it would be a lot easier if I allowed myself to fight back."

"You're a pacifist? Even when you're attacked?"

"I refuse to participate in violence. I refuse to lower myself to that level."

"I tried that," I told him. "Next time, I hit back."

"You'll turn into your own enemy."

"Maybe. I'm not as smart as you are. I don't have it all figured out theoretically. I just know that if somebody tries to hurt me, I'm going to defend myself."

He drove in silence for a little while. "Want some trail mix? There's a bag in the glove compartment."

I fished it out and poured some into my palm. It was a mixture of almonds, dried fruit, unsalted cashews, and raisins. He held out his hand, and I poured some for him. Our chewing sounded louder than normal, and each time one of us broke an almond between our teeth, it sounded like a small explosion. We were getting very close to Kiowa, and I could feel us both getting more and more nervous.

"So," he said, "I was surprised to see you walk in with Hammond. I thought he was a total loner."

"I don't really know him very well," I admitted.

"But he never seemed like a loner to me. He's a teacher. He deals with people all the time."

"Professionally, sure. But, personally, most of his close relationships are with bugs. You know that his wife left him three years ago?"

"No, I didn't know that."

"Yup. It was just when I got here. She was a real free spirit. I don't know the full story, but she ran off with another man. Hammond didn't show any visible anger. No depression. Never talked about it. Just threw himself into the world of bugs. For a while he lived in his lab. I used to think he was misanthropic, but now I see it's really sadness . . . and a little bitterness . . . so deep down, you'd never know it. And, of course, he's real shy."

I couldn't believe we were talking about the same man. "Are you kidding? He's not shy at all. I've seen him stand on a stage and speak to a hostile crowd of hundreds of people."

"He's a world-class scientist. He's used to speaking to large groups. And I didn't say he was weak — just shy. Try to really get to know him and you'll see what I mean. I feel a little sorry for him. Is this where we turn off?"

I guided Mark into Kiowa and showed him the basic layout of the town, directing him as much as possible along back streets and side streets where no one would recognize me. I pointed out the police station, the town hall, and the mill office. "Nice, rustic-looking place," he said as we cruised by Hazelwood Park. "How long have you lived here?"

"All my life."

"Parents still here?"

"Uh-huh."

"Don't want to talk about it?"

"Like you said, it's better not to ask too many personal questions."

"Okay," he said. "Remember, don't do anything today you don't want to do."

We reached the intersection of Sylvan and James McKeon Boulevard. We were fifteen minutes early. No one else had arrived yet. My heart was thumping so hard, I thought for sure Mark must be able to hear it in the silent car. "I don't think I'm gonna defy the police," I told him, and my voice came out sounding a little strange. "I'll march with you guys, but I'm not going to break the law. I don't feel good about that. I know you believe you're doing it for a good cause, but it seems to me that if everybody broke the law for their own reasons, there would be . . ."

"Anarchy?" he asked with a smile.

"Yeah, anarchy."

He parked along the mill fence and we got out. "Well, you have to realize that there's a war going on in this country." He opened the trunk and began taking out long banners and handing them to me. "Just like the Civil War, it's dividing region against region and brother against brother. Except in this war, the issue's not slavery, it's development versus environment. And the people in power, making the laws, are mostly for development. So we — on the other side — have to make our own laws. Anyway, I'm afraid we don't have time to argue the whole thing out right now. Sometime we'll sit down together and see if we can agree. Here, take this." He handed me a blue golf cap. "Pull it down low, and at least people won't recognize your face so easily."

Cars started to arrive. First, an old Volvo parked near us. Then, Dr. Eggleson cruised up in his jeep. Everyone was nervous and excited. Some people brought their own signs; others unfurled the banners that Mark had taken out of his trunk. The longest of them stretched entirely across the street and read: RESIST KIOWA MILL TREE MURDERERS. At three-forty on the dot, we began to march.

I think it was the longest mile of my life. There were twenty-five of us bunched fairly tightly together on the narrow street. I marched next to Dr. Eggleson, the two of us holding up an end of the long banner. I was scared, and Mark had admitted that these protests made him afraid, but Dr. Eggleson seemed totally at ease. Since he had taken on the mill people at the Kiowa town meeting, he was probably in as much danger as I was coming back here, but you sure couldn't tell it from looking at him. His size and calmness were comforting. I thought about what Mark had told me about him. Maybe he wasn't such a bad guy after all.

"Well, here goes," he said as we turned a corner in the road and saw the mill up ahead in the distance.

"Have you ever been in jail?" I asked him. I was embarrassed at how scared I sounded.

"Nope," he said, and gave me a smile and an encouraging pat on the back. "But there's a first time for everything. Looks like they're kind of expecting us."

A large crowd of mill workers and townspeople were waiting out in front of the mill. The men stood before the gate, blocking our way. Women and small kids stood on the other side of the street. Two camera crews were all set up to film our approach from a safe distance.

"DAMN," Mark said loudly from his place at the center of our pack. "One of our press contacts must have blabbed to the mill as soon as he got the tip. Guess he wanted a real confrontation. Well, the only thing to do now is go forward. C'mon, everybody."

We continued to march toward the gate, at a much slower pace. The fifty or so men massed there didn't budge an inch. My eyes ran over the faces in the crowd of women and kids on the other side of the street. I saw Miss Merrill and Mary Menendez. I spotted my mother on the fringe of the crowd, and pulled the bill of the blue golf cap down lower over my forehead. I guess I felt a little guilty about not even having let her know I was okay. She must have worried a lot. With my face obscured, I didn't think she could recognize me at this distance.

"Stop killing trees now. Stop killing trees now." At first it was just Mark's voice. Then other people joined his chant. "STOP KILLING TREES NOW. STOP KILLING TREES NOW." We were a hundred yards from the loggers and mill workers at the gate. Then eighty yards. The joints of my knees felt weak. Seventy-five. Once again I tasted cold, coppery fear. "STOP KILLING TREES NOW."

A voice I recognized droned suddenly from one of the police cars, amplified so that it carried above our chant. "THIS IS POLICE CHIEF CROSS. STOP. GO BACK. YOU'RE ON PRIVATE PROPERTY. I'M WARNING YOU TO STOP."

I had told Mark that I wouldn't defy the police, and now a little red warning light flashed in my brain. It was time to stop. But I was caught up in the thrill of the moment — I was chanting, my hands were grasping the banner, and my feet were rising and falling in time with the people on either side of me. I guess that's how they get soldiers to march into combat — once you feel that thrill of shared danger and you start marching with a group, you'll do almost anything before being the one to break away.

Fifty yards. Forty yards.

The loggers suddenly moved toward us. The gap closed with great speed. And then they were right in front of us, and even though I had grown up in this town and knew almost everyone, no faces or names registered. They were just a long and ominous human wall of broad-shouldered men in work clothes blocking our way.

There was a moment of silent confrontation. Someone on their side yelled: "Get the hell out of here, you longhaired punks."

On our side, I heard Mark begin the chant again: "STOP KILLING TREES NOW." A logger shoved him, but he recovered and stood his ground. Other voices on our side joined his chant: "STOP KILLING TREES NOW."

Then things happened really fast. There was a blare of sound from the police cars, and a shot was fired. At first I thought it was a bullet, but then I realized it was a tear gas cannister. A few people from our group started to run, and someone — I think a little kid — began to wail.

As if sensing weakness in our ranks, the wall of mill workers and loggers pressed forward. There were confrontations and shoving matches up and down the line. I was pushed and I stumbled back and fell to the ground for a second, but still I clung to the banner. It wasn't easy to get up again amid all the pushing and shoving and the crush of bodies, but I managed to rise to one knee. My eyes were burning and tearing, but I guess the wind had blown away most of the gas, and I could still see.

Through the moist window of tears, I suddenly saw the face and body of my father directly in front of me, looking down at me. It was almost as if he had been shrunk by his time in the hospital. He had lost weight, the lines in his face were deeply etched, and his bright black eyes gleamed out of sockets so deep, they were almost craters. I had always thought of him as burly and broad shouldered, but his musculature seemed to have dwindled by half.

He recognized me. His black eyes flashed. He took a half-step forward and raised his right hand. At first I thought that he was holding out his hand to help me up; then I realized that he was raising it to strike. He hesitated for a split second, his hand shaking. Without thinking I rose up from my knees, swung a wild right with all the force of my body behind it, and caught him flush on the point of the jaw. He went over backwards, and I blanked.

Chapter
Seventeen

When I realized where I was and what I was doing again, I found that I was running along a side street, rubbing my still-tearing eyes, and that a car was following me down the block, beeping for me to stop. I kept running — still half in a twilight world. My eyes burned, and my ears buzzed. The car kept honking. "Stop, John. Stop."

It was a voice that I recognized. I slowed and turned. Miss Merrill pulled up next to me. "I've been calling to you and honking for nearly a mile. Didn't you hear me?"

I shook my head.

"What's the matter with your eyes? Get in."

I walked over to the passenger side and got in next to her without thinking.

She drove quickly and kept silent. In less than five minutes we pulled up at a development of new garden apartments near the edge of town. The whole street was empty — no one saw her pull into the underground parking lot. She took my hand and led

169

me up a flight of stairs and down an empty hallway to her apartment.

She sat me down in a chair in the kitchen, made me tilt my head backwards over the sink, and flushed out my eyes with cold water. The burning gradually stopped. The cold water revived me a little bit — I had really been very much out of it, almost in a trance. "Better?" she asked.

"Yes. Thanks. I should go."

"Where?"

It took me about five minutes to answer that one. She stood above me, watching and waiting. My eyes roamed over her little apartment — the spices neatly arranged in their wooden rack above the stove, the spider ferns slinking up the wall, the kitchen opening into a small living room with a stereo and a beige sofa half in daylight from afternoon sun spilling in through a sliding-glass door that led to a deck. "Away."

"Away where?"

"I have to go . . ."

I started to rise, and she pushed me back down. She pulled up a chair and sat down next to me. She was wearing jeans and a light blue shirt with the sleeves rolled up to her elbows, and I could faintly smell some sort of sweet perfume — maybe lilac. She put a small and warm palm on my forehead, checking to see if I was feverish. I shut my eyes, and she held her hand there for ten or fifteen seconds. The strange buzzing that had been ringing in my ears ever since I threw the punch at my father gradually diminished.

"Stay here," she said. "At least for a while." She saw me begin to object and silenced me by brushing the hair back from my eyes in a caring gesture. "I promise I won't tell anyone you're here. Trust me. Do you trust me?"

I looked into her brown eyes and nodded.

"Good. You should lie down and take a little rest. Afterwards, we can talk, and you can figure out what to do next. Come."

A minute later I was lying down on her bed, fully clothed. She brought a blanket and spread it over me. Once again, she put her tiny warm palm on my forehead. I looked up at her. "Did you see what I did, there? That I hit my father?"

"Shhh," she said, "I saw everything. Try to rest for a little while. Just relax." She turned out the light and left me alone.

I lay in her soft bed, the woolen blanket pulled up around my chin, and drifted. The room wasn't entirely dark. A triangle of light unfolded from a small gap between the drawn curtains and the window moulding. The small bedroom had a definite feminine feel and smell — I was conscious that this was the bed Miss Merrill slept in every night. This was the bed she dreamed in. It was a soft room — extra pillows on the bed, pink curtains, even a little teddy bear.

And I had raised my hand to him. My clenched fist. And I had struck him with all my might.

The pillow was too soft. I tossed it away. Classical music was playing in a nearby apartment. I could only hear it very faintly, but it sounded like a piano concerto. The keys were dancing.

He had gone over backwards. My bully of a father, who no longer looked like a bully. . . . And even now I wasn't sorry about the punch. He had been ready to strike, and I

171

had struck first. Surely he wasn't my father anymore. Surely I wasn't his son.

My eyes moved with the piano music over the shadowy gray wall.

After a long time, Miss Merrill came in. I was surprised to see that she was wearing a fancy long blue dress. "Hi," she said softly from the door, "are you awake?"

"Yes."

She stepped into the bedroom. "I have to leave for a little while. Just a few hours. Then I'll be back."

"Where are you going?"

She walked over and sat down on the edge of the bed. "Tonight's the prom. I'm a chaperone. I'll leave early, but . . . I have to go."

I was so far removed from Kiowa High School that for a few seconds the prom didn't even register. "Oh, the prom, right," I finally said. "Go ahead. Don't worry about me."

"Will you be here when I get back?"

"Sure."

"Promise?" She looked at me and the worry showed clearly in her face.

"I promise. Don't worry. I'm not going to do anything stupid."

"Okay," she said. "I left some dinner out for you. Take whatever else you want. I'll see you later."

She gave my hand a squeeze, got up, and walked toward the door.

"Hey, Miss Merrill," I said. She turned. "Thanks for bringing me here and everything."

"You're welcome."

"Have a good time at the prom. And save the last dance for me."

"See you soon," she said and went out, closing the door behind her.

I lay there for another hour or two, my thoughts in a whirl. The classical music shut off, and the place was very quiet. I thought of the prom — a bunch of seventeen- and eighteen-year-olds dancing awkwardly to some lousy local band. Somehow I managed to feel scorn for them and to envy them at the same time.

Finally I got up out of the bed, walked into the bathroom, and took a long shower. First hot. Then I switched off the hot water and let it run freezing cold as long as I could stand it. And it was only in the shower, with the freezing water numbing my face, that I began to make decisions. Two of them, actually.

First, I would leave this town for good the next morning. The open road was the only path that made sense.

Second, when Miss Merrill came home, I would tell her how I felt about her. Why not? I had listened to her biology lessons and I had rested in her bed, and I had nothing else to lose.

She had left out a small but good dinner — some sliced steak, string beans, rice, and a salad. I ate slowly, picturing Miss Merrill in her pretty blue dress at the prom. I wondered if any of the guys would ask her for a dance. It was strange to think that my parents had gone to their high school prom in that same gym nearly thirty years ago.

The thing to do was to leave town at sunrise. I probably had six hundred dollars left in my savings account. Enough to depend on for a little while, till I found a job. Maybe San Francisco was too close. Maybe Seattle or Denver or somewhere in the Midwest. A place where no one knew who I was or what I'd done. A place far from my father, and distant from all my memories of him and of my life here.

I washed the food down with some apple juice, rinsed off my dishes, and sat down on the beige couch in the living room. It was ten o'clock. Miss Merrill would be heading home soon. I flipped through the pile of magazines on her coffee table. *Scientific American. Cosmopolitan. Time.* Nothing too interesting.

I examined the rack of CDs by her stereo system. She was a lot more hip than I was. I would never have suspected that she liked Guns n' Roses or Metallica or INXS or Ice-T. I spotted just a few of the older and slower hits that I prefer: She had Elvis's greatest hits, and some Rolling Stones and several Roy Orbison discs.

Feeling like a spy but unable to curb my curiosity, I checked her living room bookcase next. After her up-to-date and wild taste in music, I was amazed by how serious and classical her books were: Plato, Thucydides, Sophocles, Shakespeare, Darwin, etc. Then I noticed that most of the books had been bought at the Berkeley University Bookstore, presumably for college classes. Apparently Miss Merrill didn't read much on her own, for fun. Maybe she didn't have the time. Or the money. Or maybe she just wasn't a reader.

I saw two of Dr. Eggleson's books on the shelf, both with dedications to his best student. She had given them positions of honor, on the top shelf, between Darwin and Aristotle. I was willing to believe that he was a good entomologist, but I doubted that he rated such company.

I was twenty-five pages into one of Dr. Eggleson's books when I heard a key turning in the lock. I hurried to put the book back and walked toward the door to meet her. "How was the prom?"

"Fun," she said. "Silly, but fun. How are you?"

"Better."

"You seem better. Did you take some dinner?"

"It was delicious. Thanks for leaving it."

"Let me get out of this dress," she said, "and then we can talk."

She went into the bedroom to change, and I put on a collection of Roy Orbison songs. The sad, sweet, remarkable voice floated gently, like a cloud, in the tiny apartment.

She emerged from the bedroom in blue jeans and a man's long-sleeved shirt. "I see you found my music collection."

"Do you mind?"

"Not at all. Would you like a drink?"

"Sure."

"Let's see. I've got Coke. Sprite. Ginger ale."

"After the day I've had, I could use something . . . with a little punch. . . ." I said. "If you don't mind."

Miss Merrill hesitated. Then she nodded — I got the feeling she would go out of her way to try to bring up my spirits. "I think I've got a few beers. And there's some rum. How does a rum-and-Coke sound?"

"Great."

"Want to make them?"

"No, you do it." The truth was, I had never had

a rum-and-Coke in my life, and I didn't have the slightest idea how to make one.

She mixed the drinks, stirred them with a long spoon, and handed me mine. I took a sip. The Coke was so sweet, I almost didn't taste the rum.

"Good?" she asked.

"Delicious."

"You're easy to please."

We carried our drinks over to the couch and sat down. She tucked her feet underneath her knees, Indian style. We were maybe a foot apart. I couldn't help thinking that if we were boyfriend and girlfriend, we would sit like this every night. "So," she said.

"So."

"Tell me what conclusions you've come to?"

"Two," I said. "First, never listen to wise old hotel owners in San Francisco."

She smiled, and then laughed. "What?"

"I met one there who encouraged me to go home. He kept telling me that my parents would forgive and forget, and that there's no place like home. But it's not that way. This isn't my home anymore. I'm leaving tomorrow morning. That is, if you can put me up for tonight."

She sipped her rum-and-Coke. "Where will you go?"

"I've got a little money saved up. I'll go to a nice city like Portland or Seattle or Denver and find a job."

"What kind of a job?"

"You're trying to talk me out of this, aren't you?"

"I just asked what kind of a job. And what about

college? You were the best student at the high school. You can't just throw it away."

"I'll go to college eventually. There's no rush."

"That's true. But what about your high school record? If you don't take exams and finish up next year, your whole high school record will be screwed up."

I shrugged my shoulders.

"And what about your mother? Whatever problems you're having with your father, you have one of the most wonderful mothers I know. And the rest of your family . . ."

"QUIT TRYING TO TALK ME OUT OF IT."

"I'm not."

"Then what do you want from me?"

Her voice was soft, her tone calming. "You've been through a lot today, and in the past week or so. Just think things over a little more. Promise me that we'll talk again tomorrow morning. Okay?"

I hesitated. "I don't have any problem with talking."

"Good. You said you decided two things. What was the other thing?"

I took a big drink of the rum-and-Coke. She took a drink of hers.

I smiled nervously.

She smiled quizzically. Seconds ticked away.

"What was the prom like?" I mumbled.

"The band was pretty good. The decorations were hokey, but everyone seemed to have a pretty good time. I wish you could have been there."

"I'm very shy around girls."

"You have no reason to be. You're nice and smart

and very good-looking. I think a lot of girls would have been happy to dance with you."

Roy Orbison was crooning a long, slow song. I drained my rum-and-Coke, and ice cubes rattled against my teeth. "Really?"

"Really," she said.

"And what about you?" She looked at me. "I mean, did anyone dance with you tonight?"

"I danced a few times. Mostly I served punch."

I looked right into her hazel eyes. "And did you save the last dance for me?"

She didn't quite understand. "What?"

"I've never . . . I mean . . . I'm asking you to dance."

"Right now?"

I stood up and held out my hands. "I missed my prom. This is my only chance."

She shrugged her shoulders and then smiled. "You didn't miss that much. The lead singer had kind of a whiney voice, to tell the truth." She stood up and kicked off her moccasins. I kicked off my track shoes and peeled off my socks. She put one hand on my shoulder, and the other lightly on my hip. The rug felt soft underfoot. We began to waltz around the room in slow circles. I felt like a clod. "Relax," she whispered.

"How do you do the steps?"

"Two to the right, one to the left."

"My father always got on my case about my shyness with girls. Neither of my older brothers was awkward. Just me."

"You're doing fine."

We moved closer together. She put her cheek against my cheek. Each time she exhaled, I could feel her warm breath. I put my hands around her back. "Do you think I'm crazy?" I whispered.

"No, I don't think you're crazy. But you've been through an awful lot."

"Do you have a boyfriend?"

She didn't answer. Her eyes were closed, and she seemed to be lost in the music.

Our bodies pressed closely together. I could feel the curves of her hips and breasts as we swayed. For a minute or so, I lost myself in the music and the feel of her body in my arms. Then the song came to an end. We looked at each other. "Thank you," she whispered. "That was very nice."

I kissed her lightly on the lips. She didn't kiss me back, but she didn't pull away. Her eyes widened with surprise. I kissed her again, longer and deeper. Then she took a tiny step backwards. I still held her in my arms. "I love you," I told her.

"No," she said. "You're just confused. And I'm lonely. I like you, too, but . . . you're my student."

"I dropped out of school."

"I still feel like your teacher."

I smiled goofily at her. "So teach me something."

"I won't say I'm not tempted . . . but, no. Listen, you're going to make some girl very, very happy, but I just want to be your good friend. And help you through this."

I kissed her one more time, and this time when she tugged away, she pulled completely free. Her eyes were shining, and we were both breathing a little hard. "No," she said. "I'm sorry, but I mean no."

"Why? Is it Dr. Eggleson?"

She blushed and shook her head. "I am to him

what you are to me. Just his student and his friend. Now, please . . ."

I turned and walked into the bathroom, closed the door, and splashed cold water on my face. I drank some, I splashed some, and I wished I could just sink down the drain with the little whirlpool and be gone. When I finally came out, she was waiting by the bathroom door. "Are you okay?"

"Yes," I told her. "I'm leaving tonight."

"Why?"

Her question surprised me — I guess I thought it should be obvious. "Because now I've done every single stupid thing a high school guy can do in this town. Time to move on and act moronic someplace else."

She looked at me and started laughing. It's hard to sound boastfully pathetic, but somehow I had managed it. After a minute, I laughed also. It almost hurt to laugh.

"You can stay here tonight," she finally said. "You take my bed and I'll sleep on the couch. Come."

She lent me some pajama bottoms that were too short. When I was under the covers, she knocked on the door and then came in to say good-night. There was an awkward moment when she walked through the door, smiled at me, and approached the bed. "Will you be warm enough, or should I get another blanket?"

"I'll be fine."

She sat down on the edge of the bed and took my hand in her own. "John, I really don't want you to think about what happened as any kind of rejection. Because it wasn't."

"Okay," I mumbled. "Whatever . . ."

"Believe me, someday soon you're going to meet a girl your own age and really fall in love. And you'll realize that the two of us are just very good friends."

I let go of her hand. "Sure. Thanks. Good-night."

Miss Merrill stood up, but didn't walk away. I sensed there was something else she wanted to say, but she didn't know how to bring it up. When she finally spoke again, it was in a less confident, almost hesitant, tone. "John, did you talk to Dr. Eggleson about me?"

I peered up at her. Her fingers were twisting together nervously. "What do you mean?"

"The last few times I've spoken to him, he's sounded strange, and I wondered if you'd said anything to him about me?"

"Not really," I said, which I guess was a bit of a lie. "Good-night."

"Sweet dreams." She bent and kissed me lightly on the forehead, and then she was gone, pulling the bedroom door gently shut behind her. I lay awake for a long time, thinking of the past afternoon's violence, my next morning's departure, and of Miss Merrill asleep on the couch in the living room. She was only about twenty-five feet away, but a closed door and six years of life separated us. Finally I slept also.

Chapter Eighteen

The doorbell woke me. I opened my eyes and looked around — Miss Merrill was gone. From the bright sunlight shining in through the window, I saw that I had slept late. There came the sound of the apartment's front door opening and the hum of conversation. Footsteps approached. Miss Merrill poked her head into the bedroom. "John, your mother wants to see you."

"You said you wouldn't tell anyone I was here."

"I didn't. She's been frantic. She came here to ask if I could think of any place you might have gone. I wasn't going to lie to her."

I sat up in bed. I didn't know what to say.

A few seconds later, Miss Merrill ushered my mother into the bedroom. "I'll leave you two alone to talk," she said. "If you need me, I'll be outside."

My mother sat down at the foot of the bed. I was conscious that I was in Miss Merrill's bed, in just a pair of small pink pajama bottoms. My mother looked me over carefully. "This isn't the way it looks," I mumbled. "I mean, Miss Merrill picked me up after . . . what happened at the mill and brought me here. To take care of me."

"I want you to come home," my mother said. Her usually soft and friendly gray eyes were hard with a determination I had never seen before.

"Do you know what happened at the mill?"

"I saw it all. Come home."

"If you know what happened, then you know there's no way I can come. I'm sorry."

She stood up from the bed, looking down at me. "Your father is very sick."

"But he was discharged from the hospital. . . ."

"They couldn't help him. They recommended an experimental program. At the City of Hope Cancer Center. We're leaving in a week or two."

I nodded, and put my arms around my knees. "Mom, listen, I'm sorry . . . but he'll be better without me."

"Come home, John."

I thought about it — really considered going home and facing my father — and she saw the sudden anger that flashed in my eyes. "Don't you think I know about that side of him?" she asked quietly. "We got married at nineteen. Too young. I gave up a lot of things along the way. I had my dreams, just the way you have yours now." She was silent for a minute, and I thought of her painting of the cold winter landscape. "I don't have any regrets, but you mustn't think that life is easy, or that it should be easy. It's painful. It's a struggle. You make compromises. You do the best you can. He's done the best he could. There's a lot of good in the man. Come home."

I stood up out of the bed to face her. "BUT

DON'T YOU UNDERSTAND? HE WON'T WANT TO SEE ME."

"Would I be here if he didn't?"

"But . . . I want to, but . . ."

"I'll make this very easy for you," she said. "I'll wait outside for five minutes, for you to get dressed. If you're not out in five minutes, I'll leave without you. But if you don't come now . . ." Her voice quivered and broke, but she kept talking. "Don't come at all." She stepped closer and touched my cheek. "You're the baby I held in my arms seventeen years ago, but if you don't come home with me now, to see your father, don't ever come knocking on my door. Don't call me on the telephone. Don't greet me on the street. Don't ever speak to me again. I'll be waiting outside."

She left the bedroom.

I stood there for a minute or two, looking at the pattern of sunlight on the gray wall. And then I began to hunt around for my pants and shirt.

My mother let out a relieved breath when I came out of the bedroom fully dressed. She turned to Miss Merrill. "Thank you. For everything."

"All my best wishes for your husband," Miss Merrill said.

"Mom, could I talk to Miss Merrill for one second in private?"

"I'll wait out by the car."

Mom left, and I faced Miss Merrill. "Sorry about last night. I embarrassed you. And me."

"Just go home, and don't worry about it." She smiled. "If you want to know the truth, your dancing needs a little work, but you're pretty good company for such a . . . young man."

184

"Well, you're a pretty neat biology teacher," I told her. "Listen, you're wrong about Dr. Eggleson. He doesn't think of you the way you think of me. He likes you." She looked like she would interrupt me, but then she thought better of it, so I continued. "The reason he never says anything to you is that his wife left him a few years ago. He hasn't really recovered. People who know him well say he's very shy or bitter or spooked or something. So if you like him, you should go for it. Actually, I think he's a pretty cool guy for an entomologist. Bye." I held out my hand.

"Good-bye," she said, and we shook. "Good luck with your father."

"I'll need it."

I left her standing there, looking slightly perplexed, and headed out to my mother's car. The ride home took only a few minutes. Someone had cleaned all the eggs off the facade of our house. "How is he, I mean healthwise?" I asked as she pulled into our driveway.

"Weak," she said. "It's been very hard for him. He was so strong. You don't know how strong he was."

"I have some idea."

I followed her across the lawn into our house. My father was sitting in the living room rocker, wrapped in a blanket. During the ride home, I had tried to think of what I would say to him, but when I saw him in that rocker, I just froze. He looked like an old man. My mother gave me a gentle push on the back, and I walked forwards, into the room.

He looked up at me. It would have been nice if we could have had one of those happy ending father-son hugs you see in drippy movies or Life Savers commercials, but my father wasn't that kind of man. He studied me with his bright black eyes. "Sit down next to me," he finally commanded.

I sat down on the settee next to his rocker.

"Why did you set out to destroy everything I devoted my life to?" he asked in a low, steady voice.

"I didn't. Not at all."

"Everything I've built and believed in. My reputation. My friends. My town. The mill. Why?"

"I had to do what I did. It was nothing against you. I can't explain it more than that."

He rocked slowly back and forth in the rocker. "Try."

"I don't want to make you angry," I said. "I'm sorry for your illness. But what can I say? We've always been so different. We have such different values. I'm not going to apologize for the things I believe in. To me, there are things more important than even . . . this way of life. And I know I can't explain that to you."

His jaw tightened. "Goddamn, you never worked an honest day of work in your life. What gives you the right?"

I managed to stay calm. "Do you want me to leave? Because if you do, I'll go. You'll never see me again. Just say the word."

He looked at me hard and then shook his head. "You're getting a little tougher, anyway. That was a pretty good punch you threw. Where'd you learn to throw a punch like that?"

"It just happened."

"Wham, right on the jaw. Not bad."

"You admire strange things."

"I didn't think you were that strong. Or I was that weak." For a minute, his concentration drifted away. "In that hospital bed . . . I was remembering . . . what it feels like to be seventeen . . . eighteen . . . running with the football . . . breaking tackles . . . running . . ." His eyes slowly focused on me again. "It occurred to me that I had never seen a high school track meet. And that I might never get to see one."

"Why do you care about that?"

"I don't know. But I'd like to see you run."

"The season's over."

"Your team made the sectionals. Next Saturday. Just before I leave for this . . . City of Hope place."

"They won't let me run. They'll lynch me in this town if I try."

"It's not in this town."

I moved closer to him. "Listen, I'll stay with you this week. I'll talk to you. Cheer you up. Be a good son. Whatever you want. But don't ask me to run."

"Why not?"

"I'll lose."

He looked at me and then started to laugh. I watched his Adam's apple bob back and forth. "Is that what you're afraid of?"

"I'm not afraid of it. But I know it'll happen. You were an athletic hero. Glenn was. I'm not. If I've learned anything in the last week or so, it's to be honest with myself. I can't win it for you. I'm sorry."

His laugh had turned into an amused grin. "And you never came to me with that problem? It's easy to fix."

"What? You know a way for me to win?"

"Sure. I couldn't teach you much about trigonometry or French grammar, but I can help with this."

"Like there's some secret to always winning in sports?"

"Absolutely."

"What is it?"

He leaned forward. His eyes, flashing out of their deep sockets, were bright as torches. "The secret to always winning in sports is not to let yourself lose."

I thought about it. "Come on, that's not a secret. How can that help?"

"I was just about your weight. How did I set all those football records against guys twice as big? When they hit me, they wanted to break me in half. How did I always go forwards? Two thousand one hundred and eleven yards. Nobody's ever even come close. You tell me how I did it, if you're so smart?"

"I can't," I admitted.

He put his hand on my shoulder. "Thanks for coming home. I've told you what I want from you. I'm looking forward to watching you run."

Chapter Nineteen

A middle-distance runner without a sprint kick is a scared animal.

When they rang the bell for the last lap, and we swept past the roaring crowd and away into the turn, I knew I had already lost. I was barely ten feet out in front, which meant very little considering who was behind me. Tom Kellogg was running easily in second place, well within his striking distance. Joey Harrington, the returning divisional champion from St. Matthew's High, was a step or two behind Tom. They both had superb sprint kicks. A few steps behind them was a small pack of runners, several of whom probably also had the speed to overtake me.

It was hopeless.

On a good day, if I had been training conscientiously all season long, I would have tried to widen my lead right now, at the start of the bell lap. I would have let it all hang out and see if they could catch me.

But this wasn't a good day. My legs felt wooden, and my arms pumped heavily, and each breath was an ordeal. I could barely hold this pace, let alone increase it.

We rounded the turn and pounded down the back straightaway. No question, I wasn't in top form. I was surprised I could even do this well. It had been a hard week.

I had been tense all the time and I hadn't been able to train right. Since I refused to return to the high school, Miss Merrill and Assistant Principal Nichols had arranged for me to take my final exams privately. I had to do all the studying and preparing for them on my own, without the benefit of the teachers' review sessions. After studying six hours at a stretch, my eyes burned almost as badly as they had from the tear gas.

Whenever I went outside to take a break from the studying, it felt like I was taking my life into my hands. Almost overnight, Kiowa had become an angry, threatened town. A court had issued an emergency restraining order prohibiting the cutting of old growth, and the State Fish and Game Committee seemed poised to declare the butterfly a protected species. Stanley and his lawyers were fighting it every step of the way, and the case might eventually go all the way up to the cabinet-level Endangered Species Committee — the so-called "God Squad," which has the power to decide which species will be allowed to become extinct, and which species will be saved. But so far, as Dr. Eggleson had predicted, the government was siding on the side of the butterfly, and it was doing so with unusual speed.

Already, the mill had gone to one shift, and two stores on Main Street had closed. They hadn't closed because business had fallen off — they had shut down because the proprietors expected the worst and wanted to sell and get out while they still could. They had seen this same thing happen before, in other mill towns. Day by day, the fear and anger in Kiowa mounted. You could almost feel it shoot up, like the temperature of a feverish man. And when temperature gets high enough, it leads to delirium.

Violence was on the increase. Car crashes. Guys out joyriding drunk, honking horns and even shooting off guns. Our local newspaper reported three different brawls at night spots. Late one evening, a rock was thrown through our window, even though everyone in the town knew my parents were at home and understood my father's condition. When I went for walks on side streets, I was always prepared to break into a run if a hostile crowd suddenly decided to chase me. When I came to run with my old teammates in this sectional meet, not a single one of them would even talk to me.

We reached the middle of the back straightaway, and I heard Tom and Joey begin to come on. They weren't even waiting for the final hundred yards to make their move. First Tom pulled even. Then Joey. We ran step for step into the far turn, and they both began to pull away.

One step. Two.

I watched their backs. Tom ran easily, with that relaxed, loping stride that looked so effortless. Joey was shorter than I was and much more muscular. His well-developed arms shot up and down, driving his thick legs forward so that he stayed dead even with Tom.

They pulled ahead by three steps. Four.

"Don't let yourself lose," my father had said. If

that was the secret to winning at sports — if it were truly all in the mind — then why couldn't I catch them? I wanted to win as badly as they did. My father was standing at the finish line, and I wanted to break the tape in front of him more than I had ever wanted anything in my life. But I simply wasn't fast enough. It's not all in the mind. Some of it is in the legs, and the lungs.

We reached the final straightaway. The tape stretched a hundred yards or so in the distance. Tom and Joey were ten feet ahead of me now, in full sprint. I got my second wind, but all I could do was hang close.

Clearly, indisputably, my father was wrong. I couldn't win this race, just the way he couldn't outrun the grim specter gaining on him. A positive mental attitude will only take you so far, but it won't take you beyond your mortal abilities; it won't lift you beyond the grave. And it was at that moment that I accepted the fact that my father would die. Had to die. Must die. Soon. Painfully. And the unavoidable corollary: that one day I would die, too.

I had never accepted my own mortality before. The horrible truth of it became clear to me in an instant, with a fleeting vision. . . .

My mother in a black veil. Glenn and his wife, and my other brother and sisters. Me, standing awkwardly, watching a coffin being lowered into the dark earth. A few sobs.

Seventy-five yards to go. "Don't allow yourself to lose." And I came out of the momentary trance and found that I had started to gain ground. Not much. Just maybe a step. They were still almost ten feet ahead. Then nine. *Running from the specter of death itself.* Eight steps. Seven.

With fifty yards to go, Tom Kellogg faltered and lost his sprinter's pace. Joey Harrington moved cleanly into first place. Now, there were two of us chasing Joey. I closed the gap with Tom. Five feet. Four. Three. The roar of the large, sectional meet crowd came as a shot of adrenaline. I pulled even with Tom. We ran stride for stride.

Thirty yards to go. I caught a glimpse of my father standing near the finish line, his eyes on me. I ran to those flashing eyes in their deep, craterlike sockets. I ran with every ounce of willpower and manhood God had seen fit to endow me with as a birthright in my family of top-notch athletes. And for the first time since we had started racing each other in junior high school I pulled away a step from Tom Kellogg. And then two.

He fell back and then sputtered out in an instant, like a wilted autumn leaf thrown on a backyard fire.

Suddenly it was just me and Joey Harrington, the returning divisional champion at this distance, sprinting the last twenty yards for the tape. He had me by four steps. Then three. Two. I made a final lunge and actually dove at the tape, breaking the plane of the finish line a microsecond after Joey had already crossed it. The tape bowed out against his chest and then broke, and I followed him so closely that a strand of the snapped tape brushed my face as I flew forward. I rolled over and over on the track, and finally came to a stop facedown in the dust.

I lay there, sucking air, unable to get up. Runners finished their races around me. Hands took me by either arm and slowly hoisted me up. On one side it was Tom Kellogg, on the other Joey Harrington. Neither said anything. They just held me and helped me off the track. I had cut my knees by rolling over and over on the track, and blood mixed with cinders on my kneecaps and ankles.

I stood leaning against a fence, gasping. My track coach came over and shook my hand, without saying a word. Rhino walked over and broke the silence that my teammates had imposed on me: "Hell of a race. Amazing. You should be proud."

I was surprised to see Miss Merrill and Dr. Eggleson walk over. "What are you doing here?" I managed to gasp.

"We got here just before the race," Miss Merrill explained. "Hammond said it would be better to talk to you after it was over. It was thrilling, John."

"More than thrilling," Dr. Eggleson said. "What a finish!"

"Thanks," I mumbled. "Thanks for driving all the way up here."

"Oh, we're heading to San Francisco and it was right on our way," Dr. Eggleson said. "We should get going now."

I looked at Miss Merrill, and she blushed very faintly at the question in my glance. I nodded slightly. "Bye," I said. "Thanks again for coming." They walked away, and even though they weren't holding hands, you could see that it was just a matter of time.

Finally the crowd began to disperse. My father walked slowly over, and we stood facing each other.

"Sorry. I didn't win."

"No." His voice was a rasping whisper. "But you did pretty good."

"You think so?"

"I'm glad I got to see it. Very happy . . ." He shut

his mouth, apparently embarrassed by his own admission. "Listen to me, damn fool, I shouted myself hoarse."

We walked off together, and soon we were in his car, heading home. You know someone is really getting weak when you start worrying about their ability to drive. I kept glancing at my father. He held the steering wheel with both hands, and stayed in the right lane. "I've been thinking," he said. "When your mother and I leave next week for the City of Hope, why don't you go stay with Glenn?"

"What would I do there?"

"He's thinking of selling his business. Cars are like lumber in this country now. No future." He couldn't hide the anger in his hoarse voice, and for a minute or two we were both silent. "Anyway," he said, "he's thinking of opening a restaurant. He'll need help. Be a good summer job for you. And it'll be nice for me to know that you two are together." He paused to look far down the highway. "If I'm not around next fall, you might go to your senior year of high school up there, near Glenn."

"Okay," I said. "I'll think about it." The reference he had made to his own death cast a pall of gloom over both of us. The car tires gobbled up miles of highway. "Listen, are you up to something now? I'd like to try to do what you asked me before."

"What was that?"

"Explain things to you," I said. "My reasons. Are you up to it?"

"What do you want me to do?"

"Drive to the mill," I told him. "There's a hole in the fence near Highlook Lane."

Twenty minutes later, Dad pulled the car over to

the side of the road near the hole in the fence. We got out and found the gap in the wire mesh. "Now, this is gonna sound stupid," I told him, "but I've gotta blindfold you."

"Why?"

"Because of where we're going . . . I just have to."

"Then do it."

I tied a handkerchief over his eyes. "Can you see?"

"Shapes and shadows."

"That'll do. Here, take my arm." I led him off into the forest. We made slow progress. Partly it was because I was leading him; partly because he didn't have as much energy as he used to have. We skirted Thompson's Creek and headed into the thick old growth in the direction I had chased the elusive Mustard White more than a month before.

"I got to stop and rest soon," my father said after about twenty minutes.

"Almost there," I told him. "Another two minutes."

We reached the little valley with the buckeye bush that I had fallen onto and squashed. The last time I had come here, with Dr. Eggleson and Miss Merrill, about a third of the pupae had opened, and there were hundreds of blue butterflies flitting about. Now, there were thousands. "Okay," I told my father. "We're here."

He took off his blindfold and looked around. "What the hell?"

"This is the place where they live. They'll fly for a few more weeks and then start to die out. Probably some of them have already begun laying eggs."

"These things don't live anywhere else in the world?"

I shook my head.

"This is it for them?"

"Their whole species."

"Son of a bitch." He walked over to a fallen tree and sat down. I sat next to him. Neither of us said anything for a long time. It was late afternoon, and the sinking sun soaked the thick clouds a dull purple.

"Can I ask you something?" I finally said. "How come you never talk about your father or your childhood or anything like that? I mean, is there a big secret?"

"No," he said. "No secret. He was just a mean, rotten dog of a man, and I've got no reason to talk about him. We lived in a town right up on the Washington border."

"And your mother?"

"Died giving birth to me. I was raised by my father. He must've been in his fifties, but still strong as an ox. Beat the tar out of me. Fought with everyone. Drank. Gambled. Whored. Cussed. Just about the meanest sucker around. He died after a two-day drunk, and the church wouldn't let me bury him in their graveyard. So I buried him myself, up in the mountains. And then I came to live with my Uncle Mack and Aunt Lorna."

I remembered the photo of my dad as a small junior high school football player, his eyes burning with a deep-set anger. "That sounds pretty tough," I said. "Is that why you don't believe in God? 'Cause you had to go through that?"

"I don't believe in anything except hard work and old friends and family blood." After mentioning the last thing he believed in, he looked at me, acknowledging the bond and also the distance between us.

"It's too bad we've never been close. Might as well be honest about it."

I nodded. "Might as well."

"Guess it was mostly my fault."

"I always thought so."

"You sure didn't help things much."

"Anyway," I said.

"Yeah. Anyway."

"Despite all the problems, it's an honor to be your son."

"Don't start getting mushy on me, or so help me I'll pop you right here."

I smiled at him. "You might, too."

"Darned right, I might. You think just 'cause you landed one lucky punch, you can get cocky?"

"No, sir." I was grinning now.

"Second place. Damn, that boy who beat you was a midget."

"He was pretty short," I said. "But fast."

My father nodded and then coughed into his hand. "Let me tell you something," he whispered. "Dying's no fun."

"I guess not. Are you afraid?"

"Stupid question."

"Are you?"

He looked around at the sunlit little valley and the thousands of blue butterflies. "Sure," he muttered, his eyes on the treetops. "Sure I am. What the hell?" One of the butterflies had glided down and landed on his forehead. He tried to blow it away, but it clung to him with its six legs. "Get it off me, or I'll bite its head off."

I put my hand to his forehead, and the butterfly obliged by walking onto my finger. I brought it down, and he looked at it, sitting there, its wings fluttering in the breeze.

"Do those things have a name?"

"Rodgers California Blue."

He looked at me.

"They get named after the person who finds them."

"Huh," he grunted, examining the butterfly with more care. "So it carries my name?" The butterfly raised its head and looked back at him for a second. "I always expected you'd produce funny-looking grandchildren," he snarled. "But this . . . this is too much."

"It's getting dark. We should go soon."

"Just let me rest here a little more."

So I walked around the valley for a few minutes, and then I came back to get him. He sat at the edge of the fallen tree, gazing around at the cloud of blue butterflies — a strong little man who had led a hard life and had a few more months left. He turned his head when my footsteps approached. "Okay," he said. "Let's go. You don't need to blindfold me on the way out."

"But if . . . I mean . . . if they find out where this place is . . . the mill people could still come and plow over this whole valley in a few hours."

"I said you don't need to."

I didn't argue the point. I just led him out of the little valley, helped him up over the rocks, and we walked off through the trees together toward the sound of the falls in the distance.

About This Point Signature Author

DAVID KLASS is a talented author of literature for young adults. Among his acclaimed works are the novels *Breakaway Run*, *A Different Season*, *The Atami Dragons*, and *Wrestling with Honor*, an ALA Best Book for Young Adults now available as a Scholastic Point paperback.

Mr. Klass currently lives in Los Angeles, California.